WAR DOGS

NO ONE LEFT BEHIND

BOOK 2

**Wounded Warriors of the Apocalypse:
Post-Apocalyptic Survival Fiction**

AJ Newman

*

Acknowledgments

This book is dedicated to Patsy, my beautiful wife of thirty-six years, who assists with everything from Beta reading to censor duties. She enables me to write, golf, and enjoy my life with her and our mob of Shih Tzu's.

Thanks to Patsy, Wes, Richard S, David, and Richard C, who are Beta readers for this novel. They gave many suggestions that helped improve the cover and readability of my book.

Thanks to Sabrina Jean at Fasttrackediting for proofreading and editing this novel.

Thanks to WMHCheryl at http://wmhcheryl.com/services-for-authors/ for the great final proofreading and suggestions on improving the accuracy and helping me to tell a better story.

Thanks to Christian at Covers by Christian for the fantastic cover.

AJ Newman

*

Published by Newalk LLC.

Owensboro, Kentucky

*

Main Characters

Jason Walker – The main character of this story. Jason was 28 years old when the world collapsed. He joined the Army after high school. He decided to re-enlist when the Army offered to make him a Patrol Explosive Detector Dog (PEDD) Handler. He was assigned to an Army K9 unit in Europe when the SHTF. He is a bit socially backward and awkward around women. He can kill the enemy but can't deal with crying ladies.

MMax – Pronounced Max. MMax was a black and tan Belgian Malinois K9 born at Lackland AFB and assigned to Jason. He is Jason's best friend, and they've been together for two years. MMax was trained to find explosives, spot ambushes, and to neutralize enemy threats. His abilities are exaggerated a bit in this story.

Michelle Walker – Jason's wayward sister who needs to redeem herself with her family. She was an ex-drug addict and neer-do-well who began changing her life for the better when TSHTF.

SGT Maria McGill – A short, feisty Latin / Irish soldier. She was in charge of the squad Jason was assigned to in London. She and Jason had a short-lived affair. She and Jason were separated in book 1 due to the plane crash.

CPL Billy Murphy – Jason's friend and fellow soldier. He was wounded in the same explosion as Maria and Jason. "Murph" is a happy go lucky young man who is very outgoing and friendly but is an excellent warfighter.

Karen Martin – Jason saved her two daughters and her from an evil thug. She was a Biology teacher at a local high school. She became close to Jason and joined his group of survivors.

Jan Walker – Jason's mom and one of his heroes. She was a nurse and an avid gardener. She loved to run and participated in 13 and 26k marathons. Not bad for a 55-year-old woman.

Zack Walker – Jason's dad. He was a lot like Jason in appearance and demeanor. He is a prepper and competent mechanic. He disappeared before Jason returned home from the war after the lights went out but returned safely toward the end of Book 1.

Billie Johnson – Jason's mom's new friend and fellow survivor. She was a very disciplined and strict momma bear - type who is protective of her bratty kid. She is an attractive blonde-haired lady who is very defensive and hard to approach.

Katherine "Kat" Gold Kat was a small young woman who was stuck in Nashville when the SHTF. A feisty, strong-willed lady who learned how to survive and had a short fuse. Jason saved Kat from some bad men and couldn't get rid of her.

Tina – She was a liver and white Springer Spaniel who also helped save Jason's life on many occasions. She has been by Jason's side since TSHTF. Jason left her with his mom when he went to find his sister.

☆

Chapter 1

Southeast of Pleasant View, Tennessee on Highway 41.

"No. Hell, no! It's none of my damned business. MMax, I won't interfere. Why risk my life for strangers? Nope, not gonna do it." I said.

MMax just stared at me as though I'd lost my mind. Yes, I had seen the men kicking the poor man as he lay on the ground. A woman and young boy watched in terror. Then, I saw the boy jump on the man's back to save his dad. The man threw the kid to the ground and kicked him. MMax growled when the man threw the boy to the ground.

"MMax, stay!"

My eyes squinted, and my blood ran hot. I said to myself, *"Why'd that bastard have to kick the kid?. This ain't none of my business. I need to move on and find my sister."*

The man kicked the kid again, and I lost my temper. "That son of a bitch!" I raised my rifle, took aim, and squeezed off a round. The bullet hit the man's nose, and his head exploded in blood and gore. I fired twice more, and all three of the SOBs were dead or dying on the ground as their blood pooled around them.

MMax and I ran down the hill, intent on finishing off the asshats. A small limb whipped against my face drawing blood. In my haste, I didn't see a man hiding in the bushes, but MMax smelled him. MMax growled just in time for me to see the movement out of the corner of my eye. "MMax, get him!"

MMax leaped into the bushes at a full run. I heard the scream of a man who had a Belgian Malinois clamped to his arm. I yelled, "Hold him!"

The man screamed again as MMax's teeth punctured deep into his flesh. I chuckled to myself as I ran to MMax's side. The man couldn't reach his pistol with his left hand, and every time he tried, MMax shook his strong neck and set his teeth deeper into the man's arm.

I asked, "What did you plan to do with the family?"

Even in severe pain, the man remained defiant. "What the hell do you think we were going to do with them? You can have them. The young girl is prime stuff and the mom ain't half bad."

"That's what I thought," I said before I drew my knife and sliced the man's femoral artery. The asshat screamed in pain like the coward he was. I took his pistol and commanded, "MMax, out!"

"You've got a couple of minutes before you are dead. Now would be the time to pray to your God for forgiveness."

"Screw you."

I made sure the man didn't have any weapons and left him to die.

The woman tended to her husband's wounds as I walked over to them. "Is there anything I can do for you?"

She looked up and said, "No. We'll be fine once my husband catches his wind. He'll be sore and bruised, but he'll live. If you're heading north, watch for those FEMA assholes. They're rounding everyone up and placing them in camps."

I shook my head. "What if people don't need help?"

She said, "It doesn't matter. Their orders are to round up every living soul and put them to work rebuilding America."

That didn't sound right to me. As an afterthought, I asked, "Do you know what caused the apocalypse?"

"I don't know about any apocalypse, but the lights, gas, and water stopped because God wanted it to stop. He is purging the evil people from the world."

I smiled at her. "I'm leaving now. Try to avoid any more bad people."

She said, "Oh, we can't do that. The Lord wants us to spread the gospel to everyone we meet."

I caught my head shaking in disbelief. "You do know that you and your kids will be killed or taken captive if you keep walking up to strangers and telling them they're evil, don't you?"

She laughed. "It's God's work, and we must do it."

Looking back, a week had passed, and we had only made it just over halfway to Clarksville. Remember, that was less than a two-hour drive before the crap hit the fan. I got sick the first night from swallowing some water in a creek when I bathed. I threw up for the entire next day. It took three days to get over the bug, and then I was too weak to travel. MMax had never seen me this sick before, and I could tell he was perplexed by the entire situation. He stayed very close to me and whimpered a lot. I had to order him to go get him a rabbit because he wouldn't leave my side.

The next delay was caused by me sticking my nose into something I knew nothing about. We drove my dad's old truck along on Highway 41 when suddenly, a young boy jumped out in the middle of the road and blocked our progress. At first, I thought he was setting us up for an ambush. Then he yelled, "My mom's having a baby!"

I said, "What?"

"Mom's having a baby and needs your help."

"*Oh, shit, I thought.*" They didn't cover delivering puppies during my veterinary training. I said, "Take me to your mom."

The boy led MMax and me to an SUV that had been hidden in the bushes along the road. The rear driver's side door was open, and I saw legs. "Ma'am, your son said you need help."

She yelled, "Thank God! Come here, wash your hands with that bottled water, and then rinse with the rubbing alcohol. I'm a nurse, and I'll give you directions. Have you ever delivered a baby?"

"No, but I've had first aid and some veterinary training. Just tell me what to do."

The lady laughed and then calmly told me what to do, and it was a piece of cake once the head popped out. She screamed so much I was afraid people miles away could hear her. I cut the cord and tied it off as instructed, then I cleaned the baby as much as possible and laid the tiny boy on her chest. I looked at her and then at her boy. "Ma'am, where is your husband?"

She choked up a bit. "Joey, please go down to the creek and bring back a pail of water."

The small boy picked up a pail and ran into the brush. He quickly disappeared. She said, "Robert left us to find help when the car died. He never returned. I started to walk home to Smyrna, but some men killed a family not far from here. I covered Joey's eyes, but he heard the screams. The men left, and I tried to help the woman. She was dying, and there was nothing I could do to help her. She told me about the nuclear war and that the whole world was without electricity or transportation. Joey helped me push the truck into the bushes, and we've been here since the car died. I decided to wait here until after my baby was born."

I interrupted, "Could you deliver a baby by yourself?"

She replied, "I kept hoping some Good Samaritan would stop and help us. I tried to stop several families, but since I wasn't in labor, they went on their way. A Good Samaritan did stop. You are a good person."

"Sorry, I'm Jason Walker, and this is MMax. Can I take you with me toward Clarksville?"

She looked dismayed. "No, but if you could take us about ten miles south, we can stay at my cousin's home."

I took her down to her cousins, chopped some firewood, and killed a deer so they would have some meat. I was back on the road a few days later. Now you know why I need to mind my own business and get my ass up to Clarksville to find my sister.

Okay, I didn't mind helping the woman, and it was kinda neat delivering a baby. Perhaps God will remember this good deed come judgment day.

MMax and I were on a mission to find my wayward sister and take her back to the family farm. I was mission focused and didn't notice how much the earth had changed due to the grid being down and most electronics being fried. The air was crisp and clean. You could actually smell flowers and evergreens without the smell of civilization overpowering the beautiful odors. I knew this wouldn't last long, as the hint of wood fires increased every morning. Mankind would soon be deforesting the planet and choking the air with smoke from wood and coal fires. People would die from pneumonia by the droves, and lung cancer would kill many more.

MMax and I were about a mile down the road when I said, "MMax, there were some crazy assed people in this world before the crap hit the fan. Now, I think most of the sane ones must have died off."

MMax cocked his head and then licked my hand as if to say, *"I've got your back, buddy."* Well, that was my interpretation. MMax and I communicated very well. We both knew what the other was thinking and were best friends. I know I sound crazy, but MMax was a special dog and an even better friend. Yeah, I know, everyone loves their mutt and thinks theirs is unique. Mine is special.

I scratched behind his ears, and we drove on up toward Clarksville on Highway 41A North. The last known address for my sister was an apartment complex on the east side of Highway 41A in the middle of the city. This meant MMax and I would be exposed to the hazards posed by a crumbling city and its surviving population. My old truck would stand out like a diamond in a goat's ass. Thugs and police both would try to commandeer it for their own use. I decide to get as close as possible, hide the truck, and walk the last few miles to Michelle's apartment.

The area southeast of Clarksville along Highway 41A was built up with businesses and subdivisions. To avoid any potential conflict, I stopped about ten miles from Michelle's apartment and hid the truck in a barn for the night. I planned to drive further in toward her place after midnight when everyone should be asleep.

MMax and I made a cold camp and shared some Beenee Weenees, Spam, and a few crackers. MMax didn't eat much as usual since he'd gone rabbit hunting while I'd hidden the truck. He brought one back for me too, but I didn't want to start a fire. I didn't want to take the chance that someone would smell the smoke or see the flames. We settled down after supper. MMax lay on his back next to me and used his paw to move my hand to his belly. He was reminding me that I hadn't scratched his stomach for a long time. I scratched it for a while and then rubbed his belly. He moaned and wiggled in delight. A little later, I lay there with MMax's head across my stomach. I tried to think calm thoughts to help me sleep.

I tried to fall asleep but laid there thinking Maria and Murph might be in danger. I finally fell asleep but woke up dreaming about Karen. Thanks to my overactive brain and then my vivid dreams, I only caught a couple hours of shuteye but was ready to travel by one o'clock in the morning. I slid the barn doors open and stepped out into the darkness. The sheer lack of noise and the pitch-black night astounded me. There weren't any clouds, and the moon was only a sliver in the sky. The stars were breathtaking with their brilliance and shown like diamonds on a black cloth. I gazed upward for a few minutes and then prepared to leave the safety of the barn.

We were only ten miles from Clarksville, and the old truck hadn't broken down once. The truck's door opened, and I was blasted by light from the dome light. I quickly covered the light with my hand and then removed the bulb. That reminded me to take the bulbs out of the brake lights. Now, I could travel in a stealthier mode. I pulled back out on 41A and drove as slowly as I could, dodging stalled cars and debris while I watched for lights.

Again, I was amazed at how few lights there were in this suburban area. I only saw the flickering of a candle or perhaps a kerosene lamp in the distance a couple of times. I had traveled a couple of miles when I saw headlights behind me closing in quickly. I sped up to try to outrun the lights when I came around a bend and saw a fire in the middle of the road. It was a blockade.

I steered quickly off the highway into what appeared to be an industrial complex and hid behind a couple of large semi-trucks. The lights flashed by me and disappeared close to the barricade. My best guess was that we were about six miles from Michelle's apartment.

I scratched MMax just above his tail. "Well old boy, we'll have to walk on in from here."

The closest building had a street-level garage door, so I broke the window of the nearest man door and cautiously sent MMax in to check things out. He didn't alert. I followed behind him with my small flashlight enabling me to steer around pallets of boxes. I checked several of the pallets, and to my surprise; the warehouse was a paper products storage building. There were mountains of paper towels and more importantly, toilet paper.

I walked around the warehouse and didn't find anyone or any dangers. The employee breakroom was intact, so I pilfered several of the candy and food machines. The sandwich machine stunk to high heaven, but the canned soup and snack machines were half-full of edible food. I pulled the tab off a can of orange soda pop and washed down two bags of Chili-Cheese Fritos. A Hershey bar was my dessert. MMax enjoyed a can of beef stew and a bottle of water.

After eating, I brought the truck into the building and rolled the overhead door down to avoid inviting thieves. Well, maybe to keep other thieves from fighting with me to steal the food. I didn't think of MMax and myself as thieves.

"MMax, did you like the beef stew?" I asked as I held up the empty can.

MMax barked twice and wagged his tail, which usually meant yes. I loaded all the candy, chips, and canned food into the truck, along with several bundles of toilet paper. Then, as an afterthought, I filled my backpack with candy and canned food. A frown came over my face when I thought the truck could be gone when I got back with my sister.

It was now two o'clock in the morning, and everyone should be asleep. MMax and I snuck out the back door to the warehouse and cut across a field to get on a side road leading into town. We walked close to the houses and stayed in the shadows as much as possible. A cat howling in the distance was the only sound in the night until a pack of dogs joined the cat in serenading the neighborhood. There weren't any flickering candles or bonfires, other than the glow behind me from the fire at the roadblock.

A half an hour later, MMax growled and sat with his nose facing up the street. I doubted if there were any IEDs so it must be an ambush. I led MMax into the alley behind a strip mall and continued walking northwest. MMax sniffed the air and alerted again. This time, he pointed behind us. Someone was trying to sneak up behind us. Lucky for me, MMax was the best at identifying ambushes and strangers. His one weakness was the wind direction. Someone downwind could attack without much warning. MMax had magnificent hearing as well as his ability to sniff out trouble. His ears saved my ass that morning.

I dropped down in a cluster of bushes behind a house and MMax joined me. I moved behind a short wall for cover. Concealment was excellent, but it wouldn't stop a bullet. A few minutes passed, and then the sound of muffled footsteps could be heard. MMax growled just loud enough to warn me that a stranger approached.

I heard the footsteps as the person slowly shuffled their feet. A faint odor rode the slight breeze, and I saw the source. In front of me, was a small figure wearing a dark hoodie and packing a massive pistol in her hand. I say 'her' because there was just enough light from the moon to see her shape as she walked by my position. No boy had a figure like that in tight jeans, but she smelled like a sewer. Before I could decide if I wanted to approach the girl or let her disappear into the night, another shadowy figure emerged from behind her in the dark. It was a large man, about twenty feet behind her.

Crap! What to do? What to do? If I went for the man, she might shoot me. If I tried to pull her into the bushes to safety, the man might see us and shoot. I stopped thinking and yelled, "MMax, get him!" as I lunged for the girl.

I brought the young girl down with her hands pinned to her waist. She screamed obscenities at me that would make a truck driver blush. I'll only mention the milder obscenities.

"You son of a bitch, let me go. I'll cut your balls off when I get free!"

I yelled back, "I'm not going to hurt you! I saved you from a man!"

"I don't need a man to save me. Who the hell is going to save me from you? Prick!"

I struggled with her and finally got possession of the pistol only to be rewarded by a swift kick to my gonads. As I held her with one arm wrapped around her waist and my other hand covering my privates, I heard MMax doing his thing. Did I mention that she smelled horrible?

***

The stench of evil permeated the air around the man as MMax slipped up closer to him. MMax knew his human, Jason, would order him to attack this evil one, and he prepared to pounce. The order came, and MMax was only a few feet away. He saw the fire-belching gun in the human's hand and bit down on the man's arm just above his hand. MMax could taste the human's blood as he increased his bite. This man had to die, and MMax hoped his human would let him complete the mission.

MMax had killed several evil ones since the plane crash and was now on a mission to kill all of the evil ones. The woman had a neutral smell to MMax's keen sense of smell. He had never experienced this before. Humans were either good or evil from MMax's point of view.

***

I saw that MMax had caught the man by surprise and clamped down on his right arm. The man dropped his weapon and fell to the ground in agony. Every time the man tried to move, MMax bit more fiercely. The man begged someone to remove the dog.

I yelled, "MMax, hold him!"

A scream from the burly man pierced the night as MMax clamped down harder on the man's arm. The girl asked, "Who was that, your partner?"

"No. It was the man who was about to attack you. I thought you were defenseless, so I ordered MMax to attack him while I got you out of harm's way."

She said, "So, you had to attack me and grope me just to save me?"

"I didn't grope you. I saved your sorry ass from the man screaming at the other end of my dog. Calm down, and I'll let you up."

"I'll calm down when you take your hand off my left tit."

I recoiled as though I'd been hit by a train and withdrew my arm. I tried to stand up, but the girl whipped a leg around and kicked me on my shin. This pissed me off, so I lunged downward, grabbed her by the waistband of her jeans, and yanked her silly ass up in the air with her bent in double. She was a tiny thing, and I held her up with one arm.

I grabbed the wrist that was pummeling my chest and twisted it until she cried for me to stop. I said, "You may be one bad assed bitch, but I'll do what it takes to keep you from hurting me."

"I'll stop. I promise."

I lowered her to the ground but kept her wrist bent until I could pull a hank of paracord from my pocket. I forced her hands behind her and tied them together. I couldn't help but think the poor girl must be horrified, thinking she was about to be raped and abused. "Look, girl, I promise I won't hurt you if you stop trying to kill me. I'm just in Clarksville to find my sister and take her home."

"Yeah, right. That's why my hands are tied behind me with you on top of me."

"I'm not on top of you. I'm just pinning you down so you won't run."

She laughed. "So, I'm not free to go?"

"Not until we sort things out and find out why this man was following you."

I picked her up again by the waistband and helped her stand up while guarding against another kick to my balls or shin. I led her over to the man and pushed her down into a sitting position. The man begged me to release him, but I laughed in his face. I tied his feet before ordering MMax to release him, and then I secured his hands behind his back. MMax stood with his muzzle a few inches from the man's petrified face.

"Why were you stalking this little girl?"

"That ain't no little girl. She's a damned thief and a killer," the man said.

I asked, "Who did she kill?"

The girl yelled, "The bastard who stole my gun."

The man said, "She killed my buddy."

"What did your buddy do to deserve getting killed?"

"He was afraid she might hurt herself with such a big pistol and tried to trade a smaller weapon for that .50 Cal Desert Eagle. She went berserk and shot him for no reason."

I looked at the girl and saw the hood had fallen to her shoulders. She wasn't a young girl but actually a grown although small woman. "Tell your side of the story."

"My friend and I stumbled upon this creep and his friend yesterday in Clarksville. They wanted us to party with them. We told them we didn't do drugs and walked on by them. His friend followed us and tried to take my gun away. Sally tried to stop him, and he hit her with the butt of his gun. She died instantly, so I shot his sorry ass. Sally was dead, so I ran as fast as I could to getaway. Apparently, I didn't run fast enough or far enough."

Before the man could speak, I said, "Mister, if you don't want MMax chomping on you again, tell me the truth."

"My friend just wanted to…"

"MMax, watch him."

MMax moved closer to the man. "Mister, when I say the word, MMax will bite you until you tell the truth.

I'd suggest the truth, but that's up to you. MMax enjoys biting thugs and will bite you just for kicks. MMax..."

The man was terrified by now. "My friend was wrong. He did try to steal the girl's gun."

I asked, "What would he have done with the women when they were disarmed?"

A smile crept over the man's face for an instant, and then he grimaced. "Nothing, he just wanted the gun. We would have let the women go."

I pulled the massive pistol from my belt and placed it a couple of inches from the man's head. "Anything you want to say to your god?"

"Screw you and that whore."

I squeezed the trigger, the gun bucked in my hand, belched fire, and a big assed bullet took half of the man's head with it downrange. Shooting the man with the girl's gun made me feel good, but suddenly it dawned on me that the shot could be heard for miles. "What's your name?"

"Kat with a K. Short for Katherine. Shouldn't we haul ass from here?"

I cut her bindings and said, "I'm Jason. Follow me if you want to live."

☆

Chapter 2

Southeast Clarksville.

The Montgomery County Library was virtually unscathed by the riots and looting during the first weeks of the apocalypse. The employee breakroom had been ransacked, but the rest of the building was untouched. I ate a bag of potato chips and a Slim Jim. I hadn't planned on stopping for the day, but she nearly fell asleep while walking to the library. No one chased after us, and I was hungry, so we stopped at the library and spent the night.

"Kat, I'm untying you but keeping your pistol until morning. I'm putting it in my backpack, which I use for my pillow. Don't try to get it because MMax will rip your hand off. MMax, watch her."

I was tired and fell asleep knowing that MMax would let me know if Kat or any strangers were about to cause any trouble. She was a few feet away, laying on a bench. She was fast asleep. Did I mention she stank so bad it brought tears to my eyes? I rolled over and tucked my nose into my shirtsleeve. I don't know when, but I fell asleep and didn't stir much until just before dawn.

***

MMax lifted his head when he heard Kat moan in her sleep. MMax had watched her the entire time she'd slept on the uncomfortable library bench. Her smell had changed to a good person smell to him even though she'd barked at his man, Jason. She smelled like a cat but had a good person smell. She reeked with the smell of fear. This confused MMax because she barked like a ferocious person but had the stink of terror all around her. MMax wondered if Jason could smell the fear.

Kat moved and then sat upon the bench. She stood up and walked over to MMax. He gave her the low growl, but she petted his head and then knelt beside his man, Jason. She started to tug at the backpack, and MMax growled. She backed away a bit and then cuddled up to Jason's back. She fell asleep and softly snored the rest of the night. MMax liked her but wondered why she wasn't afraid of him when she stank of fear.

MMax crawled over to Jason and watched Kat through the night. He noticed the stench of fear had all but disappeared a few hours after she laid down behind Jason. She still smelled like a cat but no fear. MMax thought she wasn't afraid of Jason either, but what had caused such fear in this strong-willed human?

***

I felt a warm body curled up against my back and thought it was MMax at first until I felt her hand move across my chest and her smell slapped me in the face. I'd be lying if I said she didn't feel good against me. Her warm breath on the back of my neck felt a bit too good, but the stink was terrible. I lifted her arm and crawled away without waking her. MMax saw me get up and watched my every move. He then laid down beside the young woman. I thought this was strange. He had become closer to Karen than he ever had Maria. Now he had cuddled up to Kat. This was weird behavior for MMax or any Military Service Dog. Oh, well, MMax was no ordinary dog.

The sun had risen, and a narrow shaft of light struck the white wall behind her. It was enough to allow me to study her features. I couldn't help but look at her. She was a very petite lady who stood about five feet tall and weighed less than a hundred pounds. I didn't care for her short blonde hair that was ragged looking like someone had cut it with a butcher knife. It was short, and I liked my women to have longer hair.

She wasn't really skinny, even as small as she was. She was compact and damned good looking for such a foul-mouthed person. I noticed she was dirty and her clothes were tattered. That didn't make sense to me because clothes were plentiful now since there were probably five to six billion fewer people in the world. My gaze turned to her neck, and I saw bruises that had just about healed. Someone had tried to strangle Kat.

I knew I had missed seeing all the death and destruction from the chaos after the lights went out but had seen evidence of the death and destruction since I'd left the farm to find my sister. Every town between Clarksville and Walter Hill had been destroyed by looting and riots when the food ran out. Neighbors killed neighbors for cans of beans; however, even with all of the destruction, there were still clothes in the shops. Women would have a rough time in this new world. Kat was a tough lady, and she would have to get tougher.

I was deep in thought about Kat when MMax gave his low warning growl, which shook me out of my dazed condition. Kat stared into my eyes, and I knew I had been busted. I said, "Did you get enough sleep? You must have been worn out."

She snapped back at me. "I'm okay for someone who has been kidnapped. You were staring at me. Did you get your fill?"

"I'm sorry. Yes, I was staring at you."

I paused, and then I lied when I said, "You look a lot like my missing sister, but smell like cat crap."

She gave me the finger and turned away from me. I munched on a piece of jerky and then realized I hadn't offered her some. I offered her a part of my jerky, and she pushed my hand away.

I gazed at her face and found it to be smudged with sweat beads on her neck. "I'm sorry that I didn't offer you some food. Forgive my bad manners."

"I'm not going to beg for it or let you take it out in trade."

I was a bit caught off guard. "Ma'am, I … err … Well, that kinda shocked me. I'll share my food with you because it's the right thing to do but not because I want sex from you."

Her head dropped. "Can I please have some food?"

I dug into my backpack and pulled out a can of Beanee Weenees, a slightly crushed bag of Fritos, and a half-melted candy bar. She opened the beans and looked up at me. I saw my spoon on the table. "Sorry, I only have one spoon. You're welcome to it."

"Thanks, but no thanks."

She upended the can and allowed the beans to spill into her mouth. She took a handful of Fritos, munched on them, and then washed them down with a bottle of water I'd provided. I watched her eat and thought, *"Damn, this is the third damsel in distress I've saved in the past month. I should apply for knighthood and get a sword."*

She looked up at me, and I was caught staring into the prettiest green eyes I'd ever seen. "Do you always kidnap and gawk at women? I want my gun back."

"The women I've saved from being ravaged usually show some gratitude. Yes, you can have your gun back when I'm ready to give it back. What happened to you? Where are you from?"

Her eyes teared up, and a droplet ran down her cheek. She wiped it away with her dirty sleeve and tried to make her face look tough. She squinted her eyes and gritted her teeth. "I was in Nashville to apply for a job at Blue Sky Recording Studios. I didn't get the job and was on my way back home when the shit hit the fan. I live in a small town in Western Kentucky. Henderson has about thirty thousand people and is a nice place to live."

I asked, "If it's a nice place to live, then why leave it?"

"I'm a country western singer and hoped to get a job in Nashville while I recorded some demos. What's your story?"

"Just a minute. I was wondering how a punk rock looking young lady could make it in country western music."

Kat said, "I wear a wig and shit kicking duds on stage. My uncle used to be in Garth Brook's band before I was born, and I guess I got my love for country music from him. Now, tell me about you and your dog."

"I'm from Walter Hill, Tennessee, which is a small town southeast of Nashville. My parents, Zack and Jan, live northwest of Walter Hill and have a small farm. I was in the army in England just before the lights went out. MMax and I were on a plane home when the first EMP bombs detonated. We crashed, and I was injured. I made it home with the help of some people I met while heading there. Now I'm up here searching for my sister."

She whistled and shook her head, "Damn, you survived the war and a plane crash, just to make it long enough to die in the apocalypse."

I laughed. "MMax and I don't plan on dying. I know how to fight and protect MMax and myself. We also have each other's back. Do you have a place to go?"

Kat had a puzzled look on her face, and her lips thinned out. "I was going to head up to Henderson, but it's probably like Clarksville and destroyed."

"Don't take this the wrong way, but my mom and dad would like to add some good people to our little community. We need some hard working folks to help tend the crops and animals. We also need people who aren't afraid to fight to protect what's theirs. I know you know how to fight. Can you work from sunup to sundown? Oh, and take a bath."

Kat smiled for the first time. "That sounds inviting, but I believe I'll pass on the opportunity. I don't know you. You could be just another man like the ones I've killed. You say the right things, but it could be a ruse to make me some kind of slave."

The pint-size woman had her gall. I'd saved her scrawny butt, and she still didn't trust me. "Well, that's up to you. Here take this food and your gun," I said as I handed her several cans of soup and her pistol.

She took the food and stuck her pistol in her belt. She started to walk away but turned toward me. "Jason, there are things worse than death that can happen to a woman these days."

I said, "I'm sorry you had to experience such evil. Be careful. If you change your mind, go to Walter Hill and head northeast on the backroads. Ask around. Everyone knows my dad and mom."

She strolled away heading north but looked back a minute later to see if I watched her leave. I smiled, and she smiled back. My last thought about her was that I felt sorry for any man who tries to attack her. My balls still ached from her kick last night.

I stood there, watching her walk away and enjoyed the view. She looked over her shoulder and smiled at me. Damn, I was busted. I had Kat on my mind for a long time.

***

Kat felt Jason was a good person but had been fooled once since the bombs killed the U.S.A and didn't want to live through that again. She followed Jason and MMax from a distance into Clarksville. She heard MMax growl and point her way a couple of times when she approached too close, but Jason didn't walk in her direction. She guessed that MMax was letting Jason know they were being followed.

***

Michelle's apartment building had disappeared. In its place, was a heap of bricks, girders, and trash from three hundred families. There was no sign of Michelle.

33

Asking about her only resulted in dumb looks and a middle finger. I had to wonder if Michelle was at the bottom of the pile. She had a ground floor apartment. Tears came to my eyes as I thought about her rotting corpse at the bottom of the collapsed building. I pulled myself together and convinced myself that Michelle had survived.

The stench in the area was still overpowering. The survivors hid in the shadows, afraid to venture out in the daylight, thanks to the hoods, thugs, and crazed people suffering from drug withdrawals. The stench came from feces dumped on the streets. Yes, they dropped their shit at the curb as if a machine would come along and clean it up. Then, there were rats. Thousands of rats. I hate rats.

MMax and I also stayed in the shadows, watching for Michelle for several days without success until MMax growled. I woke up from a daydream and saw three nuns walking around the rubble with two small children. I stepped out of the shadows. "Ladies, can you help me?"

The oldest nun squared off and faced me. She said, "Sir, please go on your way and leave us alone."

It dawned on me that I had an AR, pistol, and knife, which probably scared these peaceful people. "Ma'am, I need help to find my sister. Michelle Walker. She lived in that apartment complex before the lights went out."

I noticed the other two nuns began whispering to each other, but I couldn't make out what they said. The one facing me took a few seconds, and then she said, "Come along with us. We have a dozen survivors living at our church. Your sister could be one of them. Follow us. Sorry, I'm Sister Madilyn, that's Sister Joan, and that one is Sister Grace."

I extended my hand and said, "I'm Jason Walker, and I'm pleased to meet you."

We walked several blocks before I saw the church tower up ahead. MMax was several paces in front on alert for danger, when he sat with his nose pointing to the right side of the street. He gave his low rumbling growl and looked back at me as if to check to see if I had seen the danger. I saw two young men skulking in the shadows.

Sister Madilyn walked straight at the two men and showed no fear. "You two ruffians need to move out of our way and let us go about our business. You know your boss won't tolerate you harassing us."

One of the punks walked up to the nun and slapped her, to the astonishment of the other two nuns. She fell backward to the ground. I yelled to MMax, "Get him!" as I raised my rifle and shot the second man when he drew his pistol to shoot MMax.

MMax held the man securely while I tended to the one I'd shot. I asked, "Why did you hit the nun?"

The man cried and begged God to spare him. "Help me. God, please don't let me die?"

"Answer my question!"

"Our old boss was raised in a Catholic orphanage and had a soft heart for the nuns. We killed him. Our new boss just sees them as another piece of ass."

My hand was a blur as I pulled my knife and plunged it into the man's stomach before ripping it upward. I acted without thinking or consideration for my audience. I shoved the dying man over and turned my attention to the one MMax held at bay. I took his pistol and took his knife from his belt. I told MMax, "Out," and MMax released his bite. I then said, "Watch him," and MMax stood there guarding the man.

Before I could ask him any questions, Sister Joan said, "Please don't hurt him. He's one of God's children, and we have to show him mercy."

I took my eyes off the man for a second to turn to Sister Joan, and the asshat lunged at me. He tried to take my weapon, but MMax leaped on him and bit into his throat. MMax shook the man until his blood gushed. MMax fell from the man carrying a large chunk of the man's throat with him. I was shocked. MMax was trained to bite the target's arm and subdue him.

Maxx spat the chunk of flesh to the ground and sat there looking at me as though he had fetched a ball and dropped it at my feet. When I didn't say 'Good Boy,' he had a perplexed look in his eyes. I was speechless. Both nuns were in tears as they covered the children's eyes.

It suddenly dawned on me that MMax had saved my life, which also meant he had probably saved the nuns' lives. I scratched MMax behind his ears and said, "Good boy."

MMax barked, and his whole body wiggled as he shook his tail. My approval meant a lot to MMax, and he was overjoyed that I'd liked what he had accomplished. MMax hadn't been trained to kill people who were a threat. He was supposed to hold them at bay and inflict maximum pain with his bite to their arms if they resisted. Killing people was never a goal. I knew I had to think this one over before reacting since MMax had just saved me from having to slit the man's throat.

Sister Madilyn tapped me on the shoulder. "That dog killed the poor man. Can you put him on a leash?"

I replied, "Yes," and hooked the leash to MMax. This didn't bother MMax because he was frequently on a leash during combat.

I couldn't look the nuns in the eyes as Sister Madilyn led us on to the church. She kept mumbling below her breath, and I knew I would quickly see if Michelle was with their group and leave. I wondered if the old woman would have been happier if the man had killed me instead. I looked her way, and she glared at me. I bit my tongue and didn't say anything.

We arrived and entered the rectory through a side door. A priest met us and said, "Hurry, we must hide. The gang killed Ricardo, and the new leader plans to run us out of the area. Who is your friend?"

Sister Madilyn spoke. "Father James, this is Jason Walker, and he is looking for his sister Michelle. He saved us from two of the gang members. He and that beast killed both of the men."

"Tell me more, Sister," the priest said.

Sister Madilyn gave the priest a brief rundown on the situation and made a point to tell the gruesome details about how MMax and I had killed the men.

The priest said, "Son, may God be with you. I won't judge you because the apocalypse has unleashed the wrath of many evil men. We're all warriors for God and our faith. Son, you look like you have served in the military."

I said, "Yes. I'm still in the Army. I guess it still exists."

I gave them my one-minute elevator story about how MMax and I got back to the states and then why we were here.

Father James said, "Jason, God has brought you to us at a desperate time where we need a protector who isn't afraid to get his hands dirty. We have five nuns, me, and fifteen women and children to protect from the evil men trying to harm these people. We need you to help the weak."

They were all surprised when MMax barked and nuzzled against the priest, licking his hand. The priest said, "We all have heard that God works in mysterious ways. Perhaps God has brought MMax and you to us to help us survive the evil that has been thrust upon us."

I was overwhelmed by the magnitude of what the priest had said. "Sir, I just want to find my sister and go home to safety."

Father James had a twinkle in his eyes as he said, "If we help you find your sister, will you help us go to a safe place?"

I thought, *"What the hell. If he can find Michelle, I'll do about anything."*

I said, "Look, Father, I've searched the area and can't find my sister so what will you …?"

Father James interrupted. "Sister Madilyn, bring our other two sisters here to hear what I have to say."

Sister Madilyn balked. "But we have to stay here to tend to the weak and suffering."

Father James raised his hand, "Later. Now, go!"

Sister Madilyn was angry and had a strange look on her face but left the room only to return a minute later. Father James said, "Jason, this is Sister Beth, and this is …"

The second sister looked me in the face and charged me. MMax growled ready to attack. I yelled, "Stay!" as my sister Michelle leaped into my arms.

"Jason, you've come to rescue me. Are Mom and Dad okay? What about Michael and his family; are they with mom and dad? You were in Europe! How did you get back to Tennessee?"

She nearly knocked me down, but I quickly recovered. "Sis, I'll answer all those questions after you tell me how you became a nun."

She laughed along with Father James and the other nuns. "Brother it's a long story."

★

Chapter 3

Walter Hill Tennessee

"I see an English Springer Spaniel and two young girls in the back yard. Wait. Two women are joining the girls. They're too young to be Jason's mom. I don't see anyone who could be his mom or dad," said Sergeant Maria McGill.

Murph, Corporal Billy Murphy replied, "This has to be the place. Jason told me a dozen times his dad's place was the third one on the left and about three miles up Holly Grove Road."

Maria said, "Let's get a little closer, so we can see in the house."

Maria and Murph were Jason's best friends in the Army. They were on their second tour of duty when the war broke out in Europe and spread to the United Kingdom, where they were all injured. They were lucky to have survived the explosion, and even more fortunate when they were flown back to the states before the nuclear bombs detonated. Their plane had crashed due to an EMP burst. Maria and Murph had thought Jason was dead and had left him at the crash site.

They'd traveled to Fort Campbell to report in but didn't like what they'd seen there. FEMA had set up colossal relocation camps. The tents were inside of a tall fence with piles of razor ribbon on both sides. Their homes were too far away to travel to in their condition. Both had significant wounds, and they were still recovering when they encountered the FEMA camp.

Maria had watched long enough to see the officers were taking orders from FEMA civilians and then convinced Murph to go see if they could stay with Jason's parents until they were completely healed.

***

The wind changed directions while the two soldiers snuck through the woods to get closer to the home. Tina, the springer spaniel, was guarding her new family when the wind carried their scent to her keen nose. Tina growled, sat down, and faced the direction the intruders approached from, just as Jason had taught her.

Karen said, "Tina smells something in the woods. She's alerting as though someone is approaching. Chrissy, slowly go inside and warn Zack."

A few minutes later, Zack slipped out of a window on the side facing away from the intruders. Zack kept out of sight as he worked his way around the barn to come up behind the unwelcome visitors. Zack scanned the woods. There wasn't any movement until he saw a shadow flicker in the bushes to his right. Zack raised his rifle and searched for the man. Just as he was about to squeeze the trigger, he heard, "Zack, put your weapon down. If you aren't Zack, I will blow your brains out on the grass if you pull that trigger."

Zack moved his trigger hand away from the rifle and lifted it to the sky. "How do you know me? Why are you sneaking up on my place?"

The woman said, "I'm Sergeant Maria McGill. I served with your son Jason all over the Middle East and Europe. This guy is Corporal Billy Murphy."

"Lower your rifle, and I'll answer your questions."

Maria said, "I never had my rifle aimed at you."

Zack looked at Maria first and then took a glance at Murph. "Yep, I've seen you two in several pictures Jason sent home. He's away from home to search for his sister."

"What? We thought Jason was dead!"

Zack wasn't surprised because Jason had told him he had guessed they thought he'd been killed in the plane crash. "No, he's recovered and about ninety percent. He should be back sometime this week."

"Where did he go to find his sister?"

"She's up in Clarksville. He should be back any day. Let's make you comfortable and shoot the shit."

Maria let out a deep breath. "Mister Walker, we just left Fort Campbell, and it's not a good situation. FEMA has taken over and is forcing people into relocation camps. Even what's left of the Army appears to report to FEMA."

Zack said, "But surely FEMA wants the best for our citizens and country."

Murph replied, "I certainly believe that they believe they know what's best for us; however, they're making farmers move off their productive land to work in massive FEMA community farms. The farms appear to be patterned off the Russian collective farms of the sixties."

Zack shook his head and his fists clenched. "That's about as smart as tits on a boar hog. Typical socialist dogma. Are any farmers resisting?"

"Yes, but not for long. The FEMA director sends the Army in to force the reluctant ones to comply. There have been numerous one-sided shootouts with casualties on both sides."

"Why would US soldiers turn against their own countrymen?"

Maria said, "They have been told by high ranking officers that the policy is the best in the long run for the country."

Zack was dumbfounded that this could happen in the U.S.A. He said, "Let's introduce you to the others and help you make yourselves at home until Jason returns."

Maria saw several travel trailers in the backyard. "Does anyone live in the travel trailers?"

"Yes, Jason's friends live in them. Billie and her son live in the one on the left, and Karen and her two girls live in the brown and tan one on the right. You and Murph can take the middle one until we sort things out. We think we need to attract some more of the right kind of people to join us here on our farm. People not afraid of work and not afraid of fighting when absolutely necessary," said Zack.

Maria tapped Zack on the shoulder. "We can work hard and are willing to fight to protect our friends and family. Would we be the right people for your group?"

Zack hesitated. "I want to be honest with you. I need Jason to vouch for you. From what I know about you two, you would be a great fit."

Zack introduced them to Jan before taking them out to the trailers. Jan knew of them and gave them a warm welcome. She said, "I don't like fighting and killing like Jason and you two have been forced to do, but I do realize that someone has to defend our country. We need experienced fighters to help us prepare for the bad times on the way."

Maria said, "I'll bet Jason has already worked on your OP SEC."

Jan said, "Huh?"

Murph replied, "Operational security. Posting guards, building defensive positions, securing arms and ammo, are the kind of things you do to secure your position."

Jan laughed. "Will we dig fox holes?"

Maria replied with a solemn face. "Yes, we need to have fortified positions that give cover from incoming bullets."

"Oh, my," was all Jan could say.

Zack had to tend to some chores, so Jan took Murph and Maria to the backyard to meet Karen, Billie, and the kids. Billie saw Jan approaching with the strangers and pushed Mark ahead of her to meet them. Jan said, "Billie, this is Maria and Murph. They're Jason's friends from the Army."

Billie and Mark shook their hands and welcomed them to the farm. Jan said, "We'll swap stories during supper. I'm taking them over to meet Karen and the girls now."

Karen and the girls were on the backside of the camper but heard Jan knocking. Karen came around the end of the camper and thought the two were Jason and his sister. She ran toward the man but stopped abruptly. "I'm sorry. I thought you were Jason for a minute."

Murph blushed and said, "We do look a little alike from a distance. I'm Murph, and this is Maria."

Karen hugged both as she said, "Jason has told me so much about you two! Wasn't there another soldier with you when the plane crashed?"

Maria's eyes grew wide. "Yes. John Long survived the crash but decided to go on to his home. Our homes were too far away."

"Murph and Maria, these two are my daughters Chrissy and Missy. Say 'Hi' to our new friends."

Chrissy said, "Hello. Have you seen Jason? We miss him so much and are worried about him."

Maria said, "No, we haven't seen him since we left the plane crash. We didn't think he survived. He always talked about his mom and dad's place, so we came here. Our homes are both over a thousand miles away, and we hoped to join Jason's family."

Karen said, "The decision is Jan's and Zack's on you two staying, but I like the idea."

Jan took them to the empty trailer. "You can get cleaned up and rest a bit until supper."

Jan left, and they looked at each other with sad looks on their faces. Maria said, "I can't believe we left Jason for dead. I took his pulse. He was dead."

Murph replied, "Don't beat yourself up. All three of us thought Jason had died." Murph placed his hand behind his back and crossed his fingers. "Perhaps the doctor gave him something to slow his metabolism down, or his pulse was so weak you couldn't feel it."

Maria forced a smile. "I can't get it out of my mind that we abandoned Jason."

"You have to remember. We were under attack by that crazy hillbilly with the AK47. We barely escaped alive. Damn, he only shot at me. I think he had plans for you," said Murph.

Maria hit Murph on the back of his head. "I wonder if Karen and Jason are sleeping together."

Murph snickered. "I hope so. That might give me a chance with you."

"Murph, we've had this discussion several times. You are a great big brother, but I don't think of you in the way you want."

Murph was pissed. He boiled over inside but tried to keep it to himself. "Then what about Jason? You're like a bitch in heat around him."

"Thanks for calling me a bitch. I don't know why I'm attracted to Jason. I don't want him full time, but …"

Murph wouldn't let it go because he had secretly loved Maria for years. "You want friends with benefits. Well, you saw how that woman stared at you when she heard your name. Jason has probably told her about you while they were in bed."

Maria replied, "I think you might be right about Jason and Karen. She had that puppy love look when we talked about Jason. I think Jason will choose me over a woman with two kids."

Hearing that didn't make Murph any less pissed. "So, you want to marry Jason?"

"Hell no! Jason and I are bedroom buddies, and that's all I want."

Murph went to his room and sulked for a while before a new direction leaped into his thoughts. Maria obviously didn't want him, so he was free to pursue other opportunities. His heart had been broken for a while, but he finally realized Maria had no love in her heart for him. This lifted a massive weight from him, and he was happy for the first time in years as he thought about Karen.

★

Chapter 4

The Catholic Church - Southeast Clarksville, TN.

Michelle took MMax and me to her room and pointed to a very uncomfortable wooden chair. "Sit there. Sorry, but the furnishings are a bit spartan. Does MMax need a cushion or pillow to lie on?"

"No, the floor is fine."

"So, Mom and Dad sent you to bring their wayward daughter home. What if I don't want to come home? I like it here. They treat me very well, and I like working with children and homeless mothers."

I didn't know what to say. Mom had told me that my sister still had a drug problem, but I saw a sober and well-spoken young lady in front of me. I stammered a bit and said, "You …err …seem to be …."

"Brother, spit it out. You're wondering how a druggie got sober and became a nun so quickly. I didn't even believe in God a few months ago. The damned bombs killed the grid and my drug supply. I was trying to sell myself for some Oxy when some thugs raped me and left me for dead. Sister Madilyn and Father James found me and took me to the convent. They nursed me back to health, and I've become one of them."

"Then you're not a nun, are you?"

"No. I wear the habit to keep the thugs from … well, you know what they can do to women. I don't want to become a nun, but I do want to help people. Please go home and tell Mom and Dad that I'm doing well and want to stay up here," Michelle said.

I moved to sit next to her on the bed and wrapped my arms around her. "Big Sis, I want you to have the life you want. I'll get some rest, and I'll head back home in the morning."

"Thanks, Jason. Now, tell me about you and your vicious puppy."

Michelle and I talked for hours about our lives since we'd last been together. I told her about saving a young woman. "Kat was about to be attacked. I grabbed her, and MMax attacked the man stalking her. I thought she was a teenaged girl but was surprised to find a small grown woman."

I then told my sister that I would have liked to have gotten to know Kat, but she'd left abruptly. "Sis, she was a mixture of nice and good mixed with stubborn and moody."

Michelle said, "My brother is a dumbass."

"Why am I a dumbass today?"

"You just described most of the females I know. Did you get tired of the women who just want sex without any commitment?"

"Now, wait a minute. We're not discussing my sex life."

My sister said, "Okay, let's get back to talking about killing people and MMax biting bad guys."

We were sill playfully arguing when Sister Grace called us to supper. The meal was meager at best, and I felt guilty eating their food. I fed MMax some of my jerky over their protests. The small talk centered around how thankful they were to have Michelle join them until there was a knock on the door. MMax stood up and gave his low warning growl. I told him to stay.

Father James went to the door, and we heard a man raise his voice at the Father. I jumped from my seat and was about to go help Father James when Sister Madilyn blocked my path. She said, "Let Father handle the gang. We don't need an already delicate truce to fall apart. Father James knows how to handle these poor misguided people."

The door slammed, and Father James came stumbling down the hallway from the front door. He was bent over, holding his stomach with blood running from his nose. Sister Grace helped him to a chair, and Sister Madilyn held his head back to help stop the bleeding. I asked, "Father, what happened?"

"The new gang leader doesn't believe in God or the sanctity of the church. He's giving us twenty-four hours to give up all the women and children to him, or he will attack."

Sister Madilyn said, "Surely, he doesn't mean us, nuns, also."

Father James chin dropped to his chest. "Yes, he does. He told me that if I turned you over now, he would spare any men in the church. If we wait the full twenty-four hours, he plans to kill the men and take the women."

I whispered to Michelle. "Let's take them down to Walter Hill to Mom and Dad's place."

Michelle stood up and said. "My brother has an excellent idea. Why don't we all go to our home on the outskirts of Nashville? Jason says it will be safer for us, and we can continue helping people down there."

Sister Madilyn raised her voice. "We can't leave the people of Clarksville. Many will die without us."

Father James said, "Sister, we don't have a choice. If we stay, you nuns and the other women will be abused and then be made to work in the fields after many beatings. They will kill Ed, the janitor, and me. We won't be able to help anyone. I won't order you to go, but I am going. I may not be as brave as you are, but I know if I'm dead, I can't help anyone."

Sister Madilyn said, "I'm staying."

The other nuns voted to go with us to Walter Hill. About half of the women staying in the convent voted to go to Walter Hill. I had about three or four days to figure out how to tell Mom and Dad that one priest, three nuns, seven women, and nine kids were joining our flock.

Father James and I spent an hour discussing how to sneak everyone out of the church without being detected, while the nuns and other ladies packed backpacks and shoulder bags. We were almost ready to leave when Michelle came to me. "Jason, we're gonna need a wagon to carry everything."

I went into the lunchroom and saw piles of clothes and personal possessions stacked beside enough bags to move a football team. I jumped on top of a table. "Ladies, stop and listen. You can't take all of this. We will have to walk for about five miles, and you aren't strong enough to carry these bags. We have to sneak out, so we can't use a wagon. Forget any extra clothes. Take any necessary medicine, some toiletries, water, and food. We can get clothes later."

One middle-aged woman was stuffing makeup products into a large bag. She looked up at me and glared. I pretended not to see the bag and walked on. I would have rather faced three of the gang members than tell her to pitch the crap. I probably saved my life by keeping my mouth shut.

There was some grumbling, but an hour later, the ladies and children were ready to leave. I snuck out the back door along with MMax and led the way. There weren't any asshats guarding the church. They must have thought we were too scared to leave. This was a huge break for us, and I wanted to take maximum advantage of the time before the gang realized we had fled the church. I picked up the pace and walked faster than some of the …err … less athletic women could handle.

Sister Grace said, "Could we slow down? Several of the women can't keep up."

I snapped back at her. "They need to hang in with us. We just passed Meri Court Park. We'll slow down when we get to that tall building. That puts us a mile from the church. We need to be out of the city before the gang stirs for the morning. We have four hours before the sun comes up."

I kept up the pace, and all but two stragglers stayed with the main group. Now, I walked at my usual pace, which was still too fast for the laggards. My sister begged me to slow down, but Father James said, "Jason is right. We must get far away from the gang before they start looking for us. They have several old cars that run, and they'll threaten people to make them tell if we passed by their homes."

Crap! I hadn't thought about them having working cars. I had to get them all to the warehouse and then find a trailer to haul everyone back to my parent's home. Most of the women and kids couldn't walk the eighty miles to Walter Hill. Traveling by any method was dangerous. We'd have to move after midnight but before daybreak. That only gave us four to five hours at a slow speed to travel.

We walked another mile before I stopped and gave them a ten-minute break. The lady with the large makeup bag didn't have any bags at all now. I walked past her with a grin on my face, and she gave me the middle finger salute. I said, "I'm number one! I'm number one!" and walked on past her.

Two hours later, we arrived at the warehouse. The ladies and children were leg weary but very pleased they were safe. I gathered the nuns, Father James, and my sister together and said, "I'm going out to find a trailer or another vehicle, so we can all ride to my parent's home."

Michelle said, "Let me go with you. I hate for you to be alone with all of these gang bangers searching for us."

I looked in my backpack and handed Michelle my spare 9 mm Sig. "Michelle, I know you know how to shoot. You need to stay here and protect these people. Hide if you see any strangers and only shoot as a last resort."

"But …"

I interrupted her. "Michelle, MMax, and I are trained soldiers. We know how to survive and take out the enemy if necessary. Don't worry about us. Take care of the others."

"Okay, but remember, you're still my little brother."

I looked down at her and then gave her a hug.

***

"How did they leave the church with fifty of our men and women all around the church and not seeing them?"

The man replied, "Oscar, no one thought the priest had the balls to leave the safety of the church. Manny should've posted guards instead of partying all night down by the river with most of the crew."

"Pete, Manny made two mistakes. One was not guarding the church. The other was not inviting me to the party. If I'd been invited, I would've known there weren't any guards. One more mistake and Manny will end up at the bottom of the river."

"Oscar, the men are afraid of you and don't want to bother you."

Oscar said, "They had better damned well be afraid of me. You are my second in charge. Make sure they talk with you and make sure you pass on and follow up on my orders. Now, send a team to find those people and bring the women back. Do what you want with the others."

"Boss, one of the men told me he'd seen a young man with several of the nuns the other day. He looked like a soldier. It was the same day several of our men disappeared."

"Find him and bring him to me. Dead or alive. No matter to me."

***

The sun had risen. The sky was blue, and only a few wispy clouds floated across the heavens. This wasn't a great time to be out searching for a trailer. I'm pretty good at soldier stuff, you know, marching, lobbing grenades, and killing but finding a suitable trailer in a city was tough work. Oh, I found plenty of over the road trailers. Several even had full loads of canned goods, groceries, and beer.

I saw a car dealership and broke into the showroom. I walked over to the receptionist's desk and found a phone book. A U-Haul dealer was only a block away. Even keeping in the shadows and back alleys, I was there in fifteen minutes. Right in front was a line of moving trucks and trailers. The largest trailer was a six by twelve foot enclosed cargo trailer. This one had a sign that said, "Only $69.99 per day."

I didn't plan to pay but would write an 'I owe you' note for the loan of the trailer. Now, I had to fetch my truck and get the trailer. I was only a few miles from the warehouse but was in a hurry, so MMax and I walked directly back using the streets. I scanned every door and window as I had been trained to do in combat, and MMax walked several yards ahead of me sniffing the air.

***

MMax sniffed the air and identified several good people hiding in the buildings along the way. He also smelled the stench of fear and apprehension caused by him and his human. MMax stopped suddenly. His ears perked up when he recognized the familiar smell. His eyes darted around him, and he growled when the wind shifted, and another familiar smell hammered his senses. Then he remembered; it was the smell of the man who had assaulted Father James. MMax liked Father James and wanted to bite this evil person.

MMax had caught a whiff of the good woman who smelled like a cat several times during their journey. He had alerted the first time, but since she was his human's friend, he stopped alerting.

***

I saw MMax alert. He sat, facing a building across the street. I called, "Come, MMax," as I darted behind a truck a half-second before a bullet blew a hole in the pickup's tailgate, just missing my arm. It scared the crap out of me. The sound of the shot echoed off several of the buildings, so I couldn't pinpoint where it had come from. I low crawled to the front of the truck and stuck my hat out on the end of my rifle barrel. As I'd expected but dreaded, I heard a shot, and a bullet tore through my hat.

There was another shot. Something struck the ground on the other side of the truck, and then I had instant pain. Two bullet fragments had hit my leg. One hit me on the side of my upper thigh and the other on the side of my calf. I rolled up on the curb and got behind the front wheel for protection. These asshats weren't as dumb as I'd thought. They'd figured out they could ricochet bullets into me.

Damn, I had MMax beside me behind the wheel, but a fragment hit him on the side. If we stayed there, we would be slowly bled to death. I took a couple of deep breaths and steeled myself to prepare to charge the thug on my right. Before I could move, there was a loud gun report on my right, and the asshat fell out of a window to his death. He made a thud when he hit the pavement headfirst. There were two more loud gunshots, and a man screamed. I searched the area for the great person who had saved MMax and me but didn't see anyone. I double-timed it back to the others.

Sister Grace and my sister patched MMax and me up quickly as I told them about my experience and that someone has saved MMax and me. I asked Michelle to look after the others while I drove back to get the U-Haul trailer. One of the women caught me and said, "I'm Ann Tidwell. I was an MP in the Army and have my service pistol. I'll ride with you to watch your six if Michelle watches out for my mom."

Michelle agreed, so I said, "Glad to have you. Were you on active duty when the shit hit the fan?"

"Yes, but I was home on leave. That's my mom by Father James. I was at her place when the nukes hit us. Mom hasn't come to grips with the current situation."

Her mom sat there, just staring out in space. She was in shock, and none of us knew how to treat her. I saw many more people who couldn't cope with the world falling apart during the early days. Most took their own lives. Several killed their families to protect them from the chaos. I could never understand killing your kids to protect them from bad people.

On the way over, I noticed that Ann didn't have a spare magazine for her Sig. "Ann, do you need an extra mag or some bullets?"

"Yes, if you can spare them. The short story is I had to bug out with my mom during a running gunfight. I have five rounds."

I handed her a handful of lose 9 mm rounds and a full extra magazine. "Keep these. I have some more, but we need to gather more ammo and weapons. You already know that we're in danger and could be fighting for our lives every day."

Ann had a big smile on her face as if it was Christmas. She said, "Thanks. This means a lot to me."

"Hey, I have an idea."

She asked, "What's that?"

"Could you help me train some of the women how to shoot and defend themselves? We're very short on manpower but very long on unskilled woman power."

Ann frowned. "Most of the women have skills that will come in handy for our survival, but yes, only a few have ever shot a weapon. Marge was a cop somewhere in Kentucky, Kira was on her high school's archery team, and Beth is a black belt karate instructor. She has been working with some of the women to help them defend themselves."

I saw the frown. "Look, I hope I didn't offend you. I've fought side-by-side with women soldiers and found them to be equal in battle to men. Their only weakness is upper body strength, and karate will help them with half of that issue. My concern was their lack of training and experience. We have the makings of a great little army. What was your rank?"

"Major."

I slammed on the brakes and saluted her. "Yes, Ma'am."

She nutted up, laughing as I sped back up to speed. "Jason, I'll take charge of weapons training, but I don't have as much field experience as you do, you will be promoted to captain and be in charge of our fighting forces."

"Yes, Ma'am."

"Cut that shit out. We're civilians now, and our Army days are behind us. We both have skills that are useful to the team. I think your dad will be our Commander and Chief when we get to Walter Hill, and we'll do his bidding."

I said, "You don't know my dad. Why so much trust?"

"Because you told us about him, and he wants good people to join him. I trust you and your judgment, so by extension, I trust your dad," she said.

"What you didn't say was that you trust us but will watch us closely until you're sure."

She said, "Of course."

"Same here. One can't be too careful."

We arrived at the U-Haul dealership, and I backed up to the nearest six by nine trailer while Ann watched for people. I was busy and didn't hear the sound of the truck approaching. Ann tapped me on the shoulder and said, "A vehicle is approaching. We need to bug out now."

"It's hitched, let's go," I said on the way to the driver's seat. We barely turned the corner when bullets peppered the back and side of the trailer.

Ann said, "Take the next left turn and slam on the breaks just before the turn."

I said, "But, they're on my ass."

She yelled, "Just do it!"

The turn came up, I stood on the brakes, and the small pickup careened into the back of the trailer. The collision jarred us, but neither of us was hurt. Ann began shooting as we went around the corner and hit the windshield several times. The truck bowled through a line of bushes into a parking lot. It hit a Cadillac SUV and flipped over, throwing the occupants onto the parking lot. I pushed the gas pedal down, and we sped back to the warehouse.

Michelle greeted us upon our return. "I'm glad you made it back safely, but couldn't you find a trailer with more holes. Hey, those are bullet holes! Did you run into …?

I winked and responded, "We put them into the trailer so the folks would get plenty of air."

Ann stifled a laugh. "That's your brother. He's always thinking of others. Round everyone up. We need to leave now!"

★

Chapter 5

Northwest of Pleasant View Tennessee on Highway 41.

I pulled off Highway 41 and headed south a short way on Oak Lawn Road. We had to drive during daylight to escape the gang but were now about eighteen miles from their neighborhood. We were long gone before the gang woke up, so I began to feel a bit safer. The area consisted mainly of small farms with a couple of small country subdivisions. I found a large abandoned barn and hid the truck and trailer.

I held a short meeting with everyone. I told them they needed to get some sleep and that we would drive only at night from here on until we arrived at the farm. I asked for volunteers to stand guard duty and was pleased all but two of the ladies raised their hands. Ann took the two that didn't raise their hands and had a come to Jesus meeting with them. After a brief training session, she assigned them to be our first guards.

MMax and I curled up on a stack of hay and settled in for a long nap. Of course, my mind raced from one worry to the next. What had happened to Maria and Murph? What had happened to the U.S.A? Will Mom and Dad be happy to have all of these people? I fell asleep thinking about Karen and the girls.

MMax's low growl woke me up several hours later when Ann and Michelle sat down close to me on a bale of hay. I woke up rubbing the sleep from my eyes. It must have been night outside because it was dark inside the barn. During daylight hours, there were several beams of sunlight cutting through the dust. Ann said, "Jason, it's midnight. We need to get on the road."

I said, "I need a bio break, and I'll be ready to travel."

Ann said, "I'll get everyone to load the truck and prepare to leave. We'll carry the supplies in the back of the truck and all of the people in the trailer."

I went out the back door to the barn and took care of business. The sky was dark, and clouds blocked the moonlight. Suddenly, I saw something out of the corner of my right eye that excited me and then scared me. It was a light traveling just above the treetops about a mile away. Then I heard the familiar wump, wump, wump of helicopter blades. My heart pounded as I thought this could be salvation, or FEMA trying to force people into an internment camp. I decided it would be best to avoid contact until I knew more about what they were actually doing.

I got behind the wheel with Ann riding shotgun and MMax in the middle. I said, "Did you hear the …?"

"The helicopter. Yes, it has been searching for something north of here. I thought about attracting it to us, but who knows who could have captured the helicopter or even if it is one of ours. One assumption we have to face is the U.S.A. could have also been invaded," Ann said.

I said, "Good thinking. I heard rumors about the Army working with FEMA to force people to relocate to internment camps. One guy said they even took farmers and ranchers from their land to work on big collective farms."

Ann said, "That just can't be true. I don't think our troops would do such a thing."

Michelle said, "Let's avoid them and not find out."

We drove without any lights on and only drove about thirty to forty miles an hour. We rounded a turn east of Joelton, and I saw a fire in the middle of the road. "It's a roadblock."

Ann yelled, "There are headlights behind us! Take the next right turn up there!"

I turned abruptly, and we made the turn on two wheels slinging the trailer back and forth. I felt sorry for the women and children in the trailer. I got the truck back under control when I saw another fire with a dozen people around it blocking our escape. The headlights were close behind us, and we had no side streets to escape from our pursuers. I aimed the truck up a long driveway and crashed through a fence before I hit the brakes and came to a stop. I got Michelle out of the trailer and told her, "Get in the truck and head to Walter Hill. We'll stop the gang and join you later."

"Ann, let's cover them while Michelle drives away. Michelle, we'll see you in a few days. Go to the farm."

MMax joined me as I watched the truck pull away. Ann had her pistol and jumped behind a car. I waved as Michelle drove through the back yard and then through the yard to the next street. A bullet whizzed by my head, causing me to seek cover. We carefully aimed and began killing thugs as they approached without cover. I still think to this day the bastards were high on something. A big four-wheel drive pulled up across the street, and all hell broke loose. Three or four fully automatic rifles began chewing up everything around us. I saw one of the men turn in my direction and aim a Squad Automatic Weapon at me. I ducked behind a concrete retaining wall as the 5.56 bullets ripped into the wall and the home behind me. Crap, I was pinned down.

Just when I thought I was dead, there was an explosion behind the SAW, and the man dropped dead. Then I heard a scream and silence for a minute. Three men with SAWs began strafing the wall that gave us cover. Ann said, "Shit, I've been hit."

A bullet ricocheted off something behind me, and something slammed into my head. That was the last thing I remembered about that fight.

I woke up several days later with a colossal headache and didn't see MMax or Ann. A pretty blonde nurse was changing my IVs, and a doctor and an intern were comparing notes. I sat up quickly and said, "Where's MMax?"

This scared the crap out of the nurse, and the doctor dropped his clipboard. Both doctors rushed to my bedside, and one said, "We didn't think you'd come out of the coma so quickly. What is your name?"

"I'm Sergeant Jason Walker. Where is my dog MMax?"

The doctor said, "Jason, you've had a severe injury to your head and brain. We didn't know if you'd survive, much less be speaking to us. What do you remember?"

"MMax, Ann, and I were in a firefight with some men who tried to recapture some nuns we were taking to a safe place. I was hit by several bullet fragments, then something hit my head, and I blacked out. Where is my dog?"

"Son, we only saw you and the Major in the back of the truck. The Major, or Ann, as you call her, only had a flesh wound. She reported for duty with the Army Company attached to our FEMA group. We're very short handed, and you will be a welcome addition. "

I started to let him know that I ain't staying in no damned Army when my parents and Karen could be in trouble. I chose my words carefully. "Could I see Major Tidwell? I think she can help me fill in the gaps in my memory. She also might know where my dog could be."

The doctor turned to the intern. "Charlie, go see if Major Tidwell has time to visit with the Sergeant."

***

Kat had followed Jason to make sure he was a good man before she joined his family. When she ran up across the way from Jason, she quickly saw the men hiding in the windows and took careful aim. They died, and she knew she had made a difference.

When the group pulled away in the truck and U-Haul, she climbed in the bed of the truck just before it pulled away. It was a horrible experience, but she didn't want to lose Jason and MMax. Then the chase started, and she was thrown from the truck just before Jason crashed through the yard. Kat was lucky and landed on top of some shrubs. She only received scratches and bruises. She recovered quickly and joined the fight until she ran out of bullets.

Kat tucked the large .50 caliber pistol in her waistband and searched two of the dead gang members. She found an AR15, two 9 mm Glocks, and several extra magazines. Before she could rejoin the fight, there were several explosions, and two helicopters buzzed the area, mowing the gang members down with door-mounted machineguns.

Kat moved closer to where Jason lay wounded, but two men jumped from one of the helicopters and placed Jason on a stretcher. They loaded him onto the helicopter as another man helped a wounded woman climb into the same aircraft.

Tears ran down Kat's face when she saw the helicopter take off and leave. A thought suddenly jumped into her head. She dusted herself off, searched every dead man, and gathered all weapons, ammo, and all other useable items. Kat found a place to hide her booty and then went back to make sure she hadn't missed anything.

She rolled several bodies over and found more ammunition and a couple of pistols and knives. She heard a whimper behind some bushes and drew her new Glock. Kat cautiously moved around a garage to the other side of the bushes and saw a dog trying to stand.

Kat called out to the dog. "MMax, is it you?"

The dog turned his head to Kat and lay down. Kat moved closer to MMax and placed her hand out in friendship. MMax licked her hand, so she moved closer and patted him on the head. She saw two wounds and knew she had to do something to help save his life.

***

MMax lost a significant amount of blood from his two wounds. He had been unconscious for over a week when he finally came to beside the good woman. He smelled the broth, and that woke him up. MMax lapped the salty chicken soup from the ladle and looked up to see the small blonde woman. She smelled terrible but wasn't evil. She was dirty but not evil. MMax licked her hand, and when it came to him that he couldn't smell his human, Jason. MMax became anxious and tried to move. Pain shot through his back and rear left hip. The small woman rubbed his ears and tried to soothe him, but MMax had a burning desire to be with Jason.

MMax was in pain because he'd been hit with two small caliber bullets. The broth had half a pain pill mixed in, and MMax soon fell asleep.

***

The trip to Kat's hideout was rough on her. MMax only weighed about forty-five pounds, but that was half of Kat's body weight. She was afraid someone would see them and attack since she walked so slow carrying MMax. A large pack of dogs approached from a side street, but MMax's fierce growl scared them away.

MMax laid his head on Kat's leg, and it made her feel good. She had been alone for many weeks and just having to care for MMax made her feel less lonely. She didn't have any medical training but had read a few first aide books since the shit hit the fan. She stopped the bleeding and then dug the bullet from his hip. The other shot scraped his ribs, and the bullet passed through under the skin. Kat cleaned the wounds and applied antiseptic liberally.

While waiting on the painkillers to work, she boiled some small diameter monofilament fishing line to sterilize it and then used a sewing needle and the fishing line to stitch MMax's wounds. The stitches were still painful, and MMax flinched a few times, but Kat fed him some more broth and held his head in her lap while he rested.

Kat was confused about what to do. She wanted to travel as fast as possible to Jason's father's home but felt he might not let her stay without Jason vouching for her. She also thought she had to do something to free Jason from FEMA. She hated them. Several men in black suits had forced themselves on her. It had taken several weeks, but she'd killed all of them. Kat took a nap with MMax and thought she'd decide what to do tomorrow.

Over the next two weeks, Kat watched the helicopters come and go. They always headed toward Fort Campbell, so she took MMax and went to Fort Campbell to find Jason. MMax wasn't totally healed but could walk for a few hours before long periods of rest.

***

The cute blonde nurse flirted with me that day when no one was around even though I told her about Maria and Karen. One of the orderlies told me she was an officer's woman, and he was one mean SOB. I took that to heart and didn't flirt back even though she persisted. The next day she came in with thick makeup that didn't do a good job of covering her black eye.

I flirted with her. "What happened Beautiful? You are way too pretty to have a bruise that big on your face."

"Don't flirt with me. He'll find out and finish the job. You're lucky he doesn't know I flirted with you, or he'd come in and kill you."

I behaved much better and left her alone from then on.

The next day, I saw Ann talking with my doctor before she entered the room. She looked different in the camo Battle Dress Uniform (BDU), perhaps more authoritative, I thought. She smiled when she opened the door to see if I was awake. "Jason, you look much better today. The doctors didn't give you much chance of coming out of the coma. I told them you'd been through much worse."

"Thanks, Ann. I feel like a train ran over me. Where is MMax?"

Ann looked down and gripped the bed railing. "I'm sorry, but MMax didn't make it. He was shot twice, and the rescue team thought he was dead. I know how close you were to him."

I felt tears welling up in my eyes, and I couldn't breathe. Then I hyperventilated, and alarms sounded from the machines attached to me. My doctor and several nurses rushed into the room to attend to me. I took a deep breath and remembered back when I'd first met MMax. I was in a daze. The doctor gave me a shot, and a few seconds later, I felt calm. On a scale of one to ten, my give-a-shit meter dropped to minus ten.

Ann held my hand and said, "I'm sorry about MMax."

Tears ran down my face, and I choked up.

A couple of days later, Ann came to visit me again. She wore the BDUs and now had her major's rank on her collar. She said, "Jason, you've been assigned to me. You will be my driver until you are completely healed. Then you will be assigned to one of our rescue teams as a squad leader."

I said, "What's with the BDUs? I kinda thought the Army had disbanded."

Ann replied, "Many of our troops walked away from their posts to be with their families when our nation was attacked. Our new president restructured our military and placed it under the direction of Homeland Security. Larry Nelson, the director of Homeland Security, joined the military and FEMA together and the military reports to the new FEMA director Maxine Tucker."

"Hey, hold the damned phone. That's that wacky congresswoman who wanted to disband the military because she thought the military caused us to be in so many wars."

"Yes, that's her. She's our boss."

I laughed. "Ok, you got me, and that was a good one. Now tell me what's really happening."

Ann's jaw tightened. "Sergeant Walker, I'm not laughing. The chain of command is not a laughing matter. Get your mind on your job, and don't worry about the command."

Ann wrote something on a scrap of paper and tucked it into my palm. "That's the location address for my Command Office. Tent 42A-132. Be there on Thursday at 8:00 am sharp."

Ann left the room, and a nurse walked in as she left. The nurse said, "She's all Army and stiff as a board."

I looked at the note and replied, "Yeah, I saved her life, and she reamed my ass out. But, the bottom line is that I'm a grunt who obeys orders, and it really doesn't matter who gives the orders. We have to rebuild the country."

The nurse cocked an eye in my direction and said. "Good luck with your new job. If you're ever back in my section, look me up. I think we could have a good time."

I said, "I might just do that."

I pretended to cough and swallowed the note.

Later that evening, my mind played the writing on that scrap of paper over and over. It had said, "Keep your mouth shut and do what I tell you to do, and we might get out of this alive. Nothing is what it should be, and these ain't good people. Trust no one."

I had a 'what the hell' moment, and my mind wondered what had really happened to our country and who was now in charge. I found out the answers to those questions over the next few weeks.

★

Chapter 6

Fort Campbell Kentucky

"Major Tidwell, you rose to the rank of Major after being an enlisted soldier for four years. How long have you served? I'm sorry, but as you know, we don't have any electronic records and are left with interviewing unknown personnel to decide how to use them in the best manner."

"I understand. Eleven years, sir."

"That's unheard of. You graduated from OCS six years ago and raised four ranks in five or six years. How?"

Ann said, "My MP unit was pinned down with a company of paratroopers in Belgium during a surprise attack. Every officer above me was killed early in the battle. I took charge, and we were victorious over a numerically superior enemy. The Colonel gave me a battlefield promotion to Captain. The division was cut off from supplies and support. Command left me in charge of the company until the three-month campaign was complete and then I was given my own command of a company of MPs with the permanent rank of Captain. The next year my company was in Germany when the enemy invaded from Belgium, Spain, and France.

It was a debacle for our troops. I took charge and …"

The General looked up in surprise. "Damn, now I know you. You are the Battling Bitch from Belgium. Your exploits are well known around the world. I'm pleased to meet you."

Ann shifted from one foot to the other. "Sir, a lot of what you heard has been exaggerated quite a bit."

"Didn't you receive three Purple Hearts, a Unit Citation, and a Bronze Star? There was talk of the president awarding a Medal of Honor."

"I received the Medal of Honor and was kicked upstairs in the MPs. They didn't want a Medal of Honor recipient to be killed by the enemy. I've been a desk jockey for the last year."

The General said, "I'm honored to have such a highly decorated soldier in my command. I think you will become my Colonel Curtis's XO. Colonel Curtis is in charge of our rescue and mopping up campaign."

Ann said, "I'm happy to serve in any capacity that helps our nation recover."

"Good. I do have one concern."

Ann's eyebrows rose. "Sir?"

The General said, "Your choice of a personal driver has been questioned by the officer in charge of the replacement depot. It appears that Sergeant Walker left his unit and went home like many of the other deserters."

"Sir, I can vouch for Sergeant Walker. He saved my life while on a mission to find his sister. He also saved a priest, three nuns, and a dozen other people. He and I planned to report to the nearest unit after we made sure his sister and the others were safe. We became separated from the others when the gang attacked us. Your men saved our lives."

The General snickered. "Okay, keep him. I guess you won't admit to being romantically involved with him. You don't have to answer that. Our rules have changed since the attack. The young lady outside my door is my driver and 'personal assistant'"

Ann saluted and left. She was amazed the General actually winked when he'd said, 'Personal assistant.' He drug out the word *personal* and the first three letters of *ass*-istant. The man was a creepy jerk, and Ann wanted no part of his Army.

***

A corporal met me when I left the chow hall. He told me to report to the motor pool and sign out a Humvee and then report to the main office for instructions. The vehicle looked nothing like the original Humvee. Instead, the bottom sides came together in a shallow V that was supposed to make it more bombproof. The body also had weird looking angles covered in reactive armor, which were covered in ceramic plates. It looked like it would be more at home on Mars than an Army base. Soldiers made fun of the looks but thanked God when the armor and angles saved their asses.

I disabled the autopilot and took the wheel in my hands. I'd never trusted cars that drove themselves. It was only a short drive to the Division office but long enough for me to familiarize myself with the vehicle, which was the latest model. It obviously had the improved shielding to make it CME (solar flare) and EMP proof. We needed one of these at the farm.

I parked the Humvee, but before I could report into headquarters, Ann jumped in the passenger side and said, "Sergeant, take me to the front gate."

"Yes, Ma'am. What is …?"

Ann barked, "Shut up, Sergeant! Speak when you're spoken to."

I was pissed and turned to her to give her a good cussing when she put her finger to my lips and smiled. I braked for the gate, but the guard already had the gate rising and waved us onward. Every time I started to speak, Ann put her finger to my lips. The last time, I opened my mouth and bit her finger just a bit. She smiled back and said, "No, be a good boy and wait until we find a spot to stop. I've been going crazy without you in my bed."

I was stunned until she made the slashing motion across her throat, leaned over, and whispered in my ear. "The Humvee is bugged. Play along."

I said aloud, "I know darling. I'll pull off the road as soon as we get away from the camp."

Ann gave me a thumbs up and said, "I think our Commanding Officer is fairly lenient on fraternization, but let's keep our lovemaking secret until we get the lay of the land. Up there, pull into those trees."

I made the turn, drove several hundred feet through the brush, and stopped in a secluded copse of trees. Ann pulled a Mylar blanket from her satchel and took me by the hand. "Come on, let's find a comfortable spot."

Ann made sure we were out of listening range and sight of the Humvee before placing the blanket on the ground and inviting me to sit beside her. She sat there looking at the shore of a small lake in the distance. She didn't speak. I knew part of this was an act to fool whoever was listening, but her actions led me to believe we were about to get very close.

I can't remember if I mentioned it, but Ann was about ten years older than I was and was an attractive woman, even in BDUs. I turned to her and placed my hand on her right shoulder, drawing her face toward mine. She chuckled and pulled my hand from her shoulder. "Slow down, Jason. We only have to make them think we're out here making love. We don't actually have to do it."

I replied, "Sorry, I guess I misunderstood your signals."

"You certainly did."

Blood rushed to my face as my embarrassment grew. "I already said I'm sorry. I do find you very attractive and would have told you, but we seem to always be getting shot at."

"Keep it in your pants until we get away from this phony General and FEMA, and I'll let you try your best pick up line on me. Hey, wait a minute. Weren't you trying to find that soldier Maria? I took it to mean you two were a couple."

The hole I was in got deeper. "Maria and I were friends. I miss her and want to make her safe. I don't have a wife or girlfriend, and I'm not looking for one."

Ann jumped to her feet. "That was long enough. Let's go review my soldiers at their checkpoints."

I smiled and said, "I feel used and very cheap."

Ann replied, "Good boy."

"Hey, I'm not a dog."

Ann said, "Let's cut the crap and get down to business. This is nothing but a glorified slave camp. I don't know if we can free all of them, but we need to help them and then bug the crap out of here. You need to stop complaining about the camp and put a smile on your face."

I gave her the timeout sign. "Ann, you may be the Major, but I know how to kill people and blow shit up. I agree on getting out of here, but realistically two of us can't take on the whole division."

"There are six of us, and I'll bet you'll find some of your friends in here like I did. If we just cut and run, they'll chase us down and kill us. We need a plan to blow this place up and free the slaves."

I said, "Give me a day or two to scout the place, and I'll get back to you."

"We'll inspect the entire camp over the next few days as I start my new job. I'm in charge of all of the MPs and have responsibility for law and order in the camp and perimeter security."

"The fox guarding the henhouse."

"Damn right, Skippy."

I drove Ann around the base and visited all the checkpoints at the entrances, and the ones guarding all the roads into the camp. We stopped in another copse of trees for a fake lovemaking session to continue our conversation.

Ann said, "There are four entrances and one road that passes by the front entrance. There are extra guard stations about a mile up on each side of the road to protect against surprise attacks."

I asked, "Who would attack an Army base?"

"That's a great question. The General told me there are some large gangs in the area that would love to get our weapons and vehicles."

I said, "I heard some rumors from the nurses that the General was forcing self-sustaining farmers into the camp. Perhaps he actually fears a revolt of the locals against this tyranny."

Ann replied, "I think it could be both. The General has added a rather ruthless soldier to his Rescue and Relocation group. He also just came back from the war in Europe. I believe his name is Captain John Long. The word out on Long is that he likes abusing and killing anyone who resists the relocation effort."

I frowned and clenched my fists. "I knew a Private John Long in England. He'd held every rank from private to staff sergeant several times. He was caught abusing prisoners, drinking on duty, and was accused of raping a young lady. He was in Maria's unit. We didn't like him, and Maria tried to get him booted out. I hope to God it isn't him, but I don't think he would kill innocent people."

Ann had a worried look on her face. "You'll meet him in about an hour. We're driving over to the remote compound where he's in charge of processing the newly-detained locals. There's also a sizeable prison used to contain locals who resist relocation."

Chapter 7

Fort Campbell Kentucky

MMax hid in the bushes sniffing the air. Every now and then, he caught a faint whiff of his human, Jason. He also smelled Ann's odor and knew they were together. As they circled the Fort, MMax got excited and led the short, skinny girl to a spot in the woods and sniffed the ground. The grass had been mashed down, and Jason and Ann's scent was keen. MMax couldn't bear being separated from Jason but felt danger all around. He liked the short skinny girl but loved his human.

About halfway around the camp, MMax noticed Jason's smell was the strongest yet. He tugged against the leash so hard that Kat told him to heel. MMax knew he didn't have to obey the short, skinny girl, but he liked her. He sat at her side and watched as a vehicle passed by on the road. The vehicle was a hundred feet down the road when Jason's scent blasted his snout. Ann's smell was also strong.

***

Kat saw Jason and the woman in the Humvee. She was confused, having seen Jason freely driving around the Fort. Kat had thought the worst case was that she would have to kill some guards to free Jason. Now, she only hoped Jason hadn't joined the bloodthirsty FEMA group. Kat knew firsthand about their savagery. She froze for a few seconds when MMax tugged on the leash. The flashback made her stomach queasy, and the taste of bile rose in her throat. Then a faint smile came across her face as she remembered killing the ones who had attacked her.

Kat remembered a few of the commands that Jason had used to control MMax and said, "Stay."

MMax turned and looked at Kat. She said, "Sorry, boy. We can't catch him, but I know where to find him."

Kat led MMax into the woods in front of the main gate and hid in the woods. It took several days, but she soon had a lean-to built and was ready to watch and learn. She had to know if Jason had joined her enemy or was just playing along. It was all she could do to keep MMax from charging the main gate to find his man. This was the first time MMax ever growled at her. She bent down to his eye level and said, "Trust me. We'll find Jason and get him free."

MMax lay down beside her and whimpered.

***

Ann directed me to take the Gate 7 road to Highway 41 A North. She told me to drive about four miles and turn left on Crenshaw. I made the turn and saw signs for a Walmart Distribution Center. We only drove a few hundred yards until we had to stop at a manned checkpoint. The guards recognized Ann and waved us through. She returned their salute and directed me to drive around the left side of the building and park beside several other Humvees.

That's when I saw John Long. I also saw a sergeant whipping a man with something that looked like a cat-o-nine tails from the old days. The man's back was bloody and had severe cuts made from the beads on the ends of the whip. I steeled myself as I saw John laugh. I followed Ann when she walked up to John.

"Captain Long is it necessary to beat the locals half to death for your pleasure?"

John looked up and saw Ann but didn't notice me. "Well, hello, Ma'am. We don't enjoy it, but find it a necessary evil to keep the non-complying ones in line."

Ann said. "Captain, you salute the rank, not the person. I know damn well you don't like me, but I'll bust you back down to the private you are if you don't show respect for my rank."

John saluted Ann just as he recognized me. "Well, what the hell did the cat drag in? If it isn't my friend Jason from the good old days. I ..."

I interrupted. "Who the hell promoted a laggard like you to captain? John, you never were my friend."

Captain Long said, "Major, instruct your flunky in proper military courtesy. I'll have him whipped to death if he keeps running his mouth."

I took a step toward him, and three soldiers drew their sidearms and leveled them in my direction. Ann yelled, "Lower your weapons! Sergeant Walker, apologize to the captain! Now!"

I glared at Ann and said, "Captain, I'm sorry if I disrespected your rank."

"Sergeant Walker, go to your vehicle and wait for me."

I saluted Ann and left to go to the Humvee. As I walked away, I saw a colonel, which must have been Curtis, walk up to Ann and John.

They saluted Colonel Curtis as I lingered close enough to hear the conversation. Curtis said, "Was that something I need to be involved with?"

Before Ann could speak, John said, "No, sir. Sergeant Walker and I are old friends from the European wars. He was my sergeant and gave me some good-natured shit about me being promoted to captain. He's a good man. In fact, he's too good to be a driver. I need men like that helping me to run my group."

Colonel Curtis said, "Let me talk with Major Tidwell before we make any reassignments. The General told me that Ann and the sergeant also have a history."

I heard John snicker, but Ann cut him short. "Sergeant Walker is an excellent soldier, and I also need him in my command. Sir, we can discuss the matter during our meeting this afternoon, if you like."

"Ann, that sounds good. Now, Captain, show us your operation. I hope I don't see any more of our people being whipped."

We had been on the road for about fifteen minutes, when I said, "I'm sorry."

Ann snapped back at me. "Shut up, soldier! Jason, start acting like a soldier, or you're going to get us both killed. You can't have a pissing contest with an officer in the real Army, and you know damned well these guys will kill you just for rocking the boat."

I knew she was right. I was just so mad that a man who had abused prisoners during the war had turned his evil ways on innocent people who couldn't fend for themselves. Most of the soldiers and staff I'd met were decent people. Most were afraid to speak about how the Fort was managed. They would never mention the atrocities. I had to resolve that I would play the game until we could help these people escape this prison and kill the evil leadership.

Ann saw me in the hallway after supper and passed a note to me. It said to meet her at our usual rendezvous place in the copse of trees on the north side of Hedge Row Road just below the airport. This was a great place to meet up and discuss our plans. Even if we were seen, everyone just assumed we were meeting up to make out. Little did they know there wasn't any lovemaking. It had been a long time for me, which made it tough to be so close to Ann at times.

Ann arrived a few minutes after me with her black bag and pulled out a blanket. We spread the blanket on the ground and sat next to each other. Ann reached into the bag and passed a bottle of wine and an opener to me. While I opened the bottle, Ann retrieved two stainless steel glasses. I poured us each a glass of wine, and we toasted.

Ann said, "To real friendship that will outlast this hell hole."

I raised my glass and bumped hers. "A toast to the days when we put this Army behind us and can act like regular people. And, to a beautiful woman who can probably kick my ass any day of the week."

She laughed. "And twice on Sunday. Oh, I need to mention that your friend went over the colonel's head and got you assigned to him. You start reporting to Captain Long at the end of next week."

I thought this was Ann's way of apologizing for having to dress me down in front of John and the others. Then Ann said, "Please don't put me in a position to rip you a new one again. Now rub my shoulders."

The sun had gone down. Ann unbuttoned her shirt and then flipped it down to the blanket. Darn my bad luck, she still had a sports bra on. I got behind her and massaged her shoulders. I could feel the tension in her stiff muscles, but the tension soon melted away. I kissed her neck and then trailed kisses up to her cheek. My hand wandered around to her stomach but was met with her hand, and she promptly placed my hand back on her shoulder.

"Jason, we're not having sex now and probably never will. If you can't rub my shoulders without trying to bed me, then we need to stop now."

"Ann, I just don't know how to read you. Back home after a football game in the back seat of my truck, I'd call you a prick tease."

"And you would be accurate. I enjoy the flirting but won't go much beyond that until we get out of these uniforms."

I said, "I can have you out of your …"

She chuckled. "You know damned well what I meant."

I massaged her shoulders for a few minutes more when Ann said, "Curtis is on board with our plan."

"What? I thought he was the General's man."

Ann shrugged her shoulders. "Who knows what happened between them, but I do know that your John Long was promoted to do the dirty stuff the Colonel wouldn't do for the General. Curtis hates the way FEMA and the Army are treating the civilians."

I thought for a minute. "That means we should be able to recruit new soldiers and staff quickly."

"I agree, but we must be careful to keep everything from the General and Captain Long. Long has several close allies at Fort Campbell. As a matter of fact, I have a couple of people I want you to get in good with."

Ann handed me a paper with three names. One was the blonde nurse who took care of me when I arrived here. I asked, "Why is the nurse's name on the list?"

"She's working very hard to be my friend. Buddy up to her and find out what you can. She says all the right things about joining us but, she's Long's girl. I don't think she got a choice in the matter so a little kindness will go a long way. She might turn out to be a friend, so don't go in to0 harsh." Ann said.

"Shush, I heard some bushes rustle," I said before I slipped away into the darkness.

I heard Ann whisper, "Be careful."

I looked over my shoulder, "Makes some sounds like we're making out. Draw the bastard in closer."

Ann started moaning and talking like, well, you know. I heard the bushes bristle again as I slipped up behind the person trying to catch us in the bushes. I could hear him breathing as I moved closer. The faint light of the moon told me everything I needed to know. The man in the shadows had a big knife and was ready to pounce. I caught his chin and yanked his head back while using his body to shield me from a rearward thrust of his blade. I brought my knife down from above and down between his clavicle and his rib cage. I thrust the blade back and forth to make sure I'd hit vital organs. The person fell to the ground and never made a sound.

Ann joined me and used a small flashlight to examine the man's face. It was one of John Long's men. He was one of the three men who had pointed their guns at me earlier in the day.

Ann said, "You just killed John Long's best man. Damn, you must be good at this killing stuff."

"I'm fair. Now we have to ditch this body without being seen."

Ann grabbed my shoulder. "This screws with our schedule. Leave the bastard where he lays. Get his weapons and ammo."

Damn, Ann was sure bossy. I grabbed his pistol and ammo belt, and we were on our way. "What do we do now?"

Ann ran toward the backside of the enlisted personnel tents and stopped in the shadows. She said, "The crap will hit the fan before noon tomorrow. We're not ready to take over the camp, but I think we can kill off the majority of the corrupt leadership. I need you to go get Millie and Ted. I'll get the Colonel and his men. Let's meet over by the gun range in an hour."

I found Ted first and told him about the meeting with Ann. He obviously didn't know we had to move up our plans by weeks because he was happy when I left him. I moved to the left end of the row of tents and saw Millie walking toward the supply room. I made sure no one followed her and ducked into the hallway. I whispered her name, "Millie, Millie, come here."

Before she responded, there was a sharp pain on the side of my head, and I crumbled to the ground. The blow stunned me, but I was still conscious. I heard. "I never would have guessed my woman was seeing you on the side. I'll just bang my forehead on the wall and then shoot your sorry ass. Jason Walker was a pain in my ass, and now I get revenge."

I saw him draw his gun and bounce his head on the corner of the wall. He actually laughed as blood flowed down his forehead onto his cheek. The pain didn't faze him at all. He said, "I really have to resist shooting you in the kneecaps and then shoulders. That wouldn't look like self-defense."

I saw a shadow behind him and heard a thud just before I was sprayed by his blood. Millie grunted as she hit him again with the steel hole punch. He dropped to the floor and begged for his life. She hit him repeatedly until he stopped moaning and begging for mercy. Millie said, "That will teach the bastard to beat on me."

I slowly rose from the floor and said, "Thanks. You saved my life. I didn't know you and John were seeing each other."

"We weren't seeing each other. Thanks to that worthless General, John owned me. I was his slave."

I saw her kick John in the head. "I think he's dead or dying. You can stop kicking him. Let's go. I need to get you to a meeting with Ann, and we only have a few minutes to get there."

Millie and I were the last to arrive at the meeting. Ann was in the middle of her explanation of why we had to accelerate our plans. I heard her say, "…and they'll find the body sometime in the morning …"

I interrupted and said, "Major, sorry for interrupting, but it just got worse. Millie saved my life by killing Captain John Long. He saw me approaching Millie and was jealous. He tried to kill me. She beat him to a pulp with a hole punch."

The Colonel asked, "Are you sure he's dead?"

"I didn't check his pulse, but she knocked holes in his skull. If he's not dead, then he'll be a vegetable," I replied.

The Colonel said, "Good, that was one evil piece of human garbage. Ann, you planned this turkey shoot. I have ten more loyal men and women ready to attack on your order."

Ann said, "I will take five of your men plus Ted. We'll take over the headquarters tents and kill everyone loyal to the General. Sergeant Walker will take your other five men plus a few more that he's been recruiting and kill every enlisted person we identified as loyal to the General or Captain Long."

The Colonel said, "I'll tag along with Jason to make sure the good enlisted men know that I support this coup."

Ann looked at her watch and said, "At my mark set your watches to 2100. We attack at 2300 sharp."

☆

Chapter 8

North of Walter Hill, Tennessee

Missy said, "Mom, do you really think Jason isn't coming back?"

Karen chose her words carefully. "Darling, I don't know. He was due back weeks ago, and he is a highly trained soldier. He only had to go up to Clarksville, find his sister, and return home."

Chrissy said, "Mom, we hoped you and Jason would get together. We really like him. Can't we go search for him?"

Karen replied, "Girls, Jason is a hundred times better at surviving and protecting himself than we are. All we would accomplish is getting ourselves killed or worse."

Missy had a scowl on her face. "What could be worse than …"

Chrissy punched her on the shoulder. "Darn, you're so dense. We could be …"

Karen interrupted. "Girls, we're not going, period. We need to realize that Jason might not be coming back and deal with it."

Chrissy said, "Mom, I don't like how Murph is hanging around you. I know you like Jason, and he likes you."

"Look, girls, I can't pin my hopes on a man who has been gone for several weeks in this mess of a world. Drop it and move on. I have."

***

Jan lay in bed next to her husband that night. "Zack, I overheard Karen talking with her girls."

"Babe, I'm trying to sleep."

"Karen told them that Jason isn't coming back."

"Do what? Of course, Jason's coming back. I like Karen, but I think Murph has put those thoughts in her head. He's sniffing around her like a Coon dog sniffing around a bitch in heat. Jason will come back and clean Murph's plow for fooling around with his girl."

Jan asked, "Does Karen know Jason thinks she is his girl? You know our son. He's not much for showing his feelings."

***

"Karen, Jason was my best friend in the Army, but even I've lost hope of him returning," Murph said as he wrapped his arm around her.

"I think you're right, and I do like you, but we need to go slow for my girl's sake."

Murph had a big grin. "I won't push but please don't drag it out forever."

Murph kissed Karen on the neck just as Tina began growling. Then they heard Maria call for everyone to go to their posts and prepare for an attack.

"There are a dozen people on the street looking down the driveway. Murph, let's go run them off," Maria said.

Zack wasn't happy with what she said. "Maria, let's go see what they want and determine if they're a fit for our community."

Maria smiled. "You da boss."

Zack used his binoculars to check out the people before approaching them. "Hey, there are a couple of nuns, a priest, and some women with kids. They don't look too dangerous."

Maria said, "Could be a Trojan horse."

They carried their rifles ready for action but pointed away from the people. The entire group raised their hands over their heads, and one of the nuns stepped forward. She said, "Daddy, is that you?" as she showed her bare head.

They ran the last few feet to each other and embraced in silence. After a few minutes, Zack asked, "When did you become a nun and where is Jason. Did he find you?"

Michelle's face slumped. "Jason found us and helped us escape over a month ago. I thought he would already be here. We had several killed and wounded, so we had to hole up until a few days ago. Oh shit, Jason might have been captured by that gang that tried to kill us."

"You left Jason to fend for himself?"

"Dad, I had to look out for my people and get them to safety. Jason told me to take them here, and he would join us after getting rid of the gang."

Zack was upset but knew his daughter had done the right thing. "Introduce your friends now, and we'll fill each other in on recent events later. I'm so relieved that you are safe. I love you, daughter, and I have worried a great deal about you."

"Daddy, you had a great deal to worry about. I've changed for the better. I haven't taken any drugs in months and have taken God into my life."

***

A few days later, Zack watched as Maria and Karen trained another group on how to clean their guns before they were allowed to shoot. Karen gave the pellet guns to Maria to help with training and to keep the noise down. Murph trained the other half of their group in hand-to-hand combat. He was amazed at how Michelle took to the hand-to-hand combat. Of course, she now wore civilian clothes, but the other nuns trained in their habits. Father James convinced the nuns to learn how to defend themselves. He told Zack that it would take a while to get them to handle the guns, much less becoming proficient using weapons. Sister Joan didn't want to learn anything that could harm people. She was vocal about believing that God would protect her.

Zack knew they'd been lucky so far, but luck couldn't be counted on.

Jan joined Zack during the mid-morning break and sat beside her husband under an apple tree. "Jason ain't going to be happy with Murph when he gets back."

Zack didn't reply as he watched Karen and Murph flirting across the way. Down deep in his gut, he knew something had gone wrong, and for the first time, he lost hope that Jason would ever return.

Zack heard the grass crunch as someone walked up behind him. "Zack, something is wrong. Jason should have been back by now. I know he's coming back. Jason is the toughest man I ever met," Billie said.

Zack forced a smile. "He'll be back.

"I pray every night for his return."

Jan said, "Me too."

☆

Chapter 9

Fort Campbell, Kentucky

At 22:00, the Colonel quickly introduced me to his men and women, and I was surprised that they had doubled in numbers. I recognized several of the men and had a good feeling about them. The Colonel said, "My men did a little recruiting of their own. Apparently, Captain Long made them fire on a group of preppers. Several women and children were killed along with the men. They just wanted to be left alone. They were good people."

I quickly went over the details of our plan and made a couple of modifications thanks to input from my new team. Several had experience gained in the European wars and were ready to kill to stop this madness. A few others were ready to guard the area and shoot anyone trying to stop us once the gunfire started.

I drew my knife. "Leave your rifles behind. I want you all armed with knives and a sidearm. The goal is to slip in and slit the throats of any soldier known to support the General or Captain Long. Major Tidwell will kill the General and his staff before they can wake up and sound the alarm at the same time. Shoot only as a last resort. I'll take one of you with me for tent 107. Sergeant Brown, take two men and clean out tent 108. Joe, you take 109. The rest of you guard the perimeter and have our backs."

Sergeant Brown asked, "What about the MPs guarding the Fort?"

I said, "They all report to Ann and have been told to kill anyone trying to interfere in our plans."

My grandfather's old wind up watch's second hand raced toward the fatal time the attack was to start. We snuck up on the tents a bit earlier and were in place to execute our plans. The minute hand ticked and I led my team into the tent. We each knew roughly where our targets slept. I took out the man on fire watch, and the others followed me into the tent and then spread out.

I found my first target, covered his mouth as I drew my razor sharp knife across his throat. I moved on to my next victim and was shocked to see one of my men struggling with his soldier. He yelled, "This SOB won't die! My knife is deep in …," as he held on for his life.

I ran to my next target, slit his throat, and moved to help my guy with his mark. Suddenly, the intended target stood up with my man's hands still choking him. The soldier must have been three hundred pounds and almost seven feet tall. I'd seen him around the camp. He was one of John Long's enforcers.

I yelled, "Hang on!" and then I stabbed him in the kidney since his back was turned to me and my guy was dangling on his front side. The monster hit me with a backward blow and knocked me across the room. The blow knocked the wind out of me, and I coughed and sputtered. Then I jumped up and ran toward the man ducking my shoulder just as I hit him. I struck him on the back of his knees knocking him to the ground while knocking over several bunkbeds containing sleeping soldiers. I jumped on the man, plunged my knife into his chest, and ripped upward into his heart and lungs. He rolled toward me, throwing my guy in the air on top of me. I barely missed stabbing him.

Rolling over to my feet, I kicked the man on the side of his head with my boot and then fell on him with my knife leading the way. It entered his chest between two ribs, and I yanked the handle left and right until the behemoth no longer moved. I was covered in blood as I stood up to see my team being congratulated for freeing the rest of the soldiers from the grip of John Long and the man they called 'The Mountain.'

One of the sergeants took the keys to the rifle cage from The Mountain and passed out M4s and full magazines. My little army now had thirty-three more fighters who wanted to be free from the FEMA tyranny.

I checked the other tents and only one of my people had been injured and all of the known FEMA supporters were dead. We gained over a hundred and fifty more men who wanted to join us, and three who only wanted to go home. We tied them up until Ann and the Colonel could decide what to do with them. I turned the team over to the ranking sergeant, a man I trusted and went to find Ann.

Ann, the Colonel, and several other officers stood in front of the General's office. Ann saw me and waved for me to join them. She asked, "How did your operation go?"

Before I could answer, I came into the light, and they saw the blood covering my face and uniform. Ann's hands raised to her face in shock. The Colonel said, "I hope that's not your blood."

I laughed and said, "Most of it belongs to 'The Mountain.' I didn't realize how big the beast was, or I would have assigned several soldiers to kill him. He beat Rodrigues and me pretty bad. Sorry, sir, the mission was successful, and we now have over a hundred and fifty more soldiers ready to join your team."

The Colonel said, "Our part of the operation was also successful. The General, his men, and all of the crooked FEMA people are dead. We have a few clerks and such to keep an eye on. Ann, take Sergeant Walker to the medics and get him patched up. We'll meet again at 0600. I doubt if anyone will be able to sleep but try to get a few hours rack time. That's an order."

***

I started to talk when Ann said, "Let me speak first. Jason, I was afraid for your life when I saw the blood. I knew I liked you, but now I know I have strong feelings for you. Let's get you patched up and see where this goes."

The medics performed a quick examination of my body and sent me to the showers to wash the blood away. A few minutes later, I came back wearing only a towel. The head doctor looked me over and said, "You are bruised and battered, but only have a few scrapes and cuts. The nurse will give you a couple of shots and a bottle of antibiotics. You'll be sore for a week, but you'll be okay. I want to say that my staff and I are happy to be free of the General and those sick FEMA SOBs. Thank your men for us."

I shook his hand, and he and the nurses left Ann and me in a private room. A minute later, a nurse brought a fresh uniform to the door. Ann took the uniform and placed it beside me on the table. She locked the door from the inside and came to me. We embraced and kissed for several minutes. Things were getting hot and steamy when she shucked her uniform and joined me on the narrow examination bed.

Unfortunately, for my sex life, I said, "Ann, I can't wait for you to meet my parents. We need to leave in the next day or two, so they won't think I'm dead."

Ann rose up and looked down at me. "Hon, I can't leave my new command so soon. They need me, and we need to expand this operation and clean out any other crooked FEMA operations. Please stay with me."

It was then; I realized Ann and I were never meant to be together. I had to get back home and protect my family. Hell, I didn't even know if my sister had made it home. I also had to go find my brother and his family. I looked up into Ann's eyes. "Can't we talk about that in the morning?"

I saw a tear running down her cheek, and then she lay down on my chest. We lay there for an hour, both knowing that I would go home, and she would go on serving our broken country. I felt lousy laying there with her because I knew that I didn't care for her as much as I did for Karen. Then it occurred to me that I lusted for Karen but didn't care for her any more than Ann.

Damn, I really didn't know what I wanted. I'd been a soldier most of my adult life and took pleasure where I found it. Karen was different. She stirred a longing in me to settle down and make a steady life. I just wished we'd talked about how we'd felt for each other.

As if she'd read my mind, Ann rolled off me to the floor and dressed. I said, "Ann, I'm sorry, but I have to go home."

She bent down and kissed me. "Jason, I always knew we would never be seriously involved. You need a woman to have kids with and settle down with a family. I'm going to have a squad of MP's escort you most of the way back home. We have some old farm trucks that are in excellent shape. One of them will be ready to go by 0900. You can leave with the escort any time after that."

I started to kiss her goodbye, but she said, "No, a clean break is best. Good luck and I'm very sorry about MMax."

The commotion at the fort caused MMax to growl to alert Kat, who was asleep. He tugged at his leash, so Kat put her boots on and took him out to see what was going on. They snuck up to the fence line, only about twenty-five yards from where Jason's smell was the strongest. She hid in a low spot when she spotted two soldiers walking toward them. She told MMax to be quiet and listened. The soldier closest to her said, "I can't believe we're free from the General and FEMA. Will you stay or go home?"

The second soldier replied, "I'm going home. I'll go with the group that escorts Sergeant Walker south to the Nashville city limits. The Colonel gave him a truck and some supplies plus the escort. It's the least he could do since Walker fought and killed 'The Mountain.'"

"Did you see how bloody that fight was?"

"Yep, but Walker only got beat up. 'The Mountain' got stabbed a dozen times before he died."

Kat homed in on the statements about the truck and Jason driving home. She watched a soldier drive an old pickup and park it close to Jason's tent. She ran back to her hideout with MMax to find the wire cutters and her backpack. Kat knew it was risky, but she was going to cut the fence and try to find Jason.

Kat led MMax by the leash back to the fence and tied the leash to it while she cut a hole large enough for MMax and her to enter the fort. The hole was finally large enough, so she crawled through, and MMax followed. There was a glow in the eastern horizon that told Kat she only had a few minutes to stow away in Jason's truck. She walked to the truck with MMax and looked in the truck's bed. *"Great,"* she thought. The supplies had a canvas tarp over them. She helped MMax into the vehicle by lowering the tailgate. MMax jumped in, and she climbed under the tarp with him. Kat reached back and lifted the tailgate. It made a loud clank when it closed.

As she feared, she heard a flurry of voices, and then the tarp was ripped open and bright light blinded her. She heard, "What are you doing? Why are you hiding in this truck?"

She heard Jason shout. "What's going on out there?"

Jason rounded the corner of the tent at the same time MMax heard his master's voice and leaped from the truck. MMax barked and ran into Jason, knocking him down. One of the guards thought Jason was being attacked, so he drew his pistol and aimed it at the dog. He pulled the trigger just as Kat knocked his arm away.

The shot rang through the camp, waking everyone close by them.

It only took me a second to realize MMax had tackled me. MMax wasn't dead! MMax licked me all over as I tried to hug him. I called out, "It's okay. This is MMax, my dog and that's Kat. I know her."

By this time, Kat was also in my lap with MMax. She hugged me and babbled on about what had happened since I had lost track of MMax. I saw Ann rush up and her eyes widened when she saw the cute blonde in my lap. She said, "MMax is still alive! Jason, I'm so happy for you! Who is your other friend?"

I said, "Oh, this is just Kat. I saved her from some thugs a while back. She saved MMax and cared for him until he recovered from the wounds. I owe her for saving my best friend."

Ann said, "I see. If she can climb off of you, we need to discuss your departure."

I moved Kat off my lap and stood up, still holding on to my dog. I said, "Come," and MMax followed me to Ann's quarters. Ann gave me a hug and said, "I'm going to miss you."

"Ann, you mean a lot to me. You helped me survive the camp and kept me from doing some stupid stuff."

Ann replied, "But I don't mean enough for you to stay with me?"

"Or you could say that you don't care enough about me to go home with me."

Ann asked, "Are you and the girl romantically involved?"

"Hell, no! She hates my guts. She tried to kill me when I saved her life."

Ann laughed. "She didn't look like she wanted to kill you a few minutes ago."

"I don't know where that came from. When I met her, I thought Kat was just a skinny and dirty little boy. She's had a rough go of it. Several of the FEMA people raped and abused her, right after the lights went off."

"Are you taking her home with you?"

"I really don't know. I offered to take Kat to our village, but she left on her own."

Ann replied, "Do you mind if we get her some clean clothes and a shower? She stinks."

I said, "I wouldn't tell her she stinks. She has a short fuse."

"How old is she? Should she have a pistol?"

I laughed, "I think she's about twenty-two. She's got a chip on her shoulder …"

Ann snickered, "And a short fuse."

***

Kat hadn't had a real bath in over a month. Living in abandoned buildings and alleys for months was bad enough, but the bad men were the worst. The stink and dirt had kept several men from pursuing her. She hated the smell of the mixture of cat poop and her own pee.

She enjoyed the hot water and scented soap. It reminded her of better days. Her mom would go nuts if she saw Kat's butchered hair, chipped nails, and clothes. Especially the clothes. Her mom had given her two credit cards when she'd turned sixteen with a $20,000 limit just for clothes and gas for her Corvette and Jeep. There was nothing but the best for the daughter of the CEO of Women's World Magazine.

She didn't recognize the person who stared back at her in the mirror. Her previously perfect locks were now scalloped and ragged. She'd lost five pounds from an already slim five-foot-nothing body. All of her bones stuck out. She combed her hair and thought she looked too much like a skinny tomboy.

This was a far cry from her days in college and spending time at her father's country club. She'd led a life of privilege and hadn't wanted for anything. Even when she tried to break away and have a singing career, her mom and dad bought her clothes and made her take money. Kat put the money in the bank and then waited tables and sang at honkytonks in Nashville to make a meager living. She'd had to learn fast and adapt to this cruel apocalyptic world. Some of the lessons had left deep scars.

There were two sets of clothes and underwear lying on the counter, along with a small bag of makeup. Kat quickly dressed in a blouse and matching shorts and found a pair of sneakers and socks under the counter.

The person in the mirror stared at her, and she thought that she now looked okay. Too darn skinny, but regular meals would take care of that. Then she shuddered because she had tried to look dirty and like a boy to keep the perverts and thugs from noticing her. She smiled because MMax and Jason would protect her. She would finally be safe.

Kat removed her fancy wallet and a few other personal possessions from her pants. She opened the wallet and pulled out the driver's license. The picture looked like her but had a smile. Katherine T Gold the license said. It also said she was five feet tall and weighed a hundred and two pounds. Kat threw her old clothes away but kept her boots. She stuck her knife and pistol into the waistband of her shorts and was ready to meet the world.

★

Chapter 10

North Central Tennessee on Highway 41 South

The old Ford F250 bounced along on the debris covered road. Limbs and gravel covered the road in many places. A storm had recently devastated the area, and I could still smell the ozone and smoke from the lightning strikes. I saw entire neighborhoods flattened by what must have been a string of tornadoes. We had to backtrack a couple of times to get around massive fallen trees. I had never given much thought to encountering a disaster in the middle of an apocalypse.

MMax sat between Kat and me in the front seat of the old 1973 pickup. She almost looked normal now with her hair combed and clean clothes. Not to mention, she smelled like a woman should smell now. She caught me looking at her. "What ya looking at?"

I grinned. "A clean girl who doesn't stink. You clean up real good. Still a bit short and skinny but at least no dirt caked on your face."

"Well, you didn't smell so good yourself when I first met you," she said.

I looked at her and then said, "How old did you say you were?"

"I'm twenty-one and will be twenty-two this August. I know I look much younger. You should have seen the bartender's face when I showed him my ID for my first legal drink."

I said, "I'm surprised he didn't say it was a fake ID and throw you out."

She laughed, "My dad and his buddy, the police commissioner, were with me."

I started to speak when a utility pole fell across the road a few feet in front of us. My reflexes took over, and I downshifted and pushed the pedal down hard. The front tires hit the pole, and we were thrown upward with only our seat belts keeping our necks from being broken. Then there was an immediate repeat from the back tires. Half of our cargo flew out of the truck's bed onto the road behind us.

There were two loud impacts as bullets hit the tailgate and then the front of the bed. I also heard multiple gunshots coming from behind us. We hurled around a bend, and I stopped behind an abandoned truck. "Kat stay in the truck and take off if I don't …"

Darn her hide, MMax, and she ran to me ignoring my order. I gave up and ran through the woods to see if I could help my friends fight off the attackers. We were too late. I poked my head around a tree and saw one of the attackers kill the last of the squad. My heart raced when one man pointed up the road to where we had gone, and several men got in the Humvee. I grabbed Kat and ran for our lives.

We jumped in the truck and thank God, it fired right up. I squealed tires taking off and drove as fast as the truck would go until I saw a narrow dirt road up ahead on the right. I made the turn on two wheels and immediately looked for a place to hide the truck. I saw an opening in the tall brush and shot into the tangled mess where I slid to a stop, jumped out of the vehicle, and cut a couple of brushy limbs. "Kat, help me erase our tracks."

We used the limbs to rake our tracks, and there was no longer any evidence we had turned off. I just hoped they weren't smart enough to look for tire tracks in the dirt and decayed leaves. We hid behind the truck and heard the Humvee roar down the road. We waited with guns ready; however, we didn't see the Humvee again.

"Kat, stay hidden in the bushes with MMax while I go back and check for any survivors."

She pulled at my arm. "No, there could be more of them. Use your head. We saw them shooting the last man in the head while he laid helpless on the ground. They're all dead."

"Kat, our motto is 'No man left behind.' I have to go back and make sure. I know I can't bury them, but I have to make sure there are no survivors."

Kat dropped my arm and climbed into the truck with MMax. "Let's go."

I started to tell her to stay behind but realized she wouldn't listen. I also liked the idea of her covering me while I checked for survivors. "Okay, let's go but do what I say."

A massacre is the only way I could describe the scene. The men and women from the first Humvee were spread out on the ground. All but one had been executed after being wounded. The big surprise was there was a third Humvee with a massive tree on top of it. The tree crushed the top down almost to the floorboard. Everyone was dead. The passenger side door had buckled away from the vehicle exposing a twisted body.

I screamed, "Oh, no!" and fell to my knees.

I hugged her limp body until I felt a hand on my shoulder. Kat said, "Jason, we need to get out of here. They will be coming back to salvage supplies, ammo, and Humvee parts. Bring her body, and we'll bury it later."

I had to pry her body from the vehicle. I couldn't leave her to rot in the wrecked Humvee. Kat gave me a blanket, and I placed her in the back of the truck. I guess I was in shock for several hours because I couldn't remember finding Ann's body.

Kat took the wheel and drove south on 41A until she took Highway 249 over to Highway 24 East. I was in a daze but tried to keep watch for danger. I saw a sign ahead and told her to get off Highway 24 and to work over to Highway 109. I knew we had to avoid Nashville and populated areas as much as possible.

Kat pulled off the road where Highways 178 and 258 crosses. She carefully drove into a stand of trees on the southwest corner, so we could bury Ann. Kat said, "I think you can find this place again if you ever want to visit her grave."

We didn't have a shovel but found a tire tool and a hubcap to dig the shallow grave. I placed Ann's body in the grave and said the Lord's Prayer before covering her. We spent the next two hours scrounging for rocks to cover the shallow grave. I couldn't bear thinking that animals would dig her up.

We camped there for the night with Kat huddled up to my side and MMax's head on my stomach. I couldn't sleep at all that night as my mind replayed my memories of Ann. Our little growing community at Walter Hill could sure use an experienced leader like her. She died trying to make sure I got home safely.

I laid awake and heard every cricket chirp, every mosquito buzz my face, and every dog that barked that night. Sleep evaded me until the sun glowed below the horizon. I tried counting to a million and got to 187,994 before I got bored and gave up. You don't believe me. It's true. Try it sometime when you can't sleep. It almost always works. Almost.

I don't know when I fell asleep, but I woke up to the smell of fried Spam and BBQ beans. One eye peeked through my lashes and saw Kat cooking. The smell of the wood smoke mixed with the Spam and beans made my mouth water. "What's for breakfast?"

Kat chuckled, "Do you mean lunch, sleepyhead?"

"What time is it?"

Kat moved to me and lifted my left wrist. "Your old watch says it's 12:21."

"I can't believe I slept that long," I said.

Kat scooped some beans and Spam into an empty can and said, "Eat."

I slowly stood up. "I have to take care of business first. Where's the TP?"

She pointed, and I was on my way to the bushes. I went to the other side of the truck and down the hill a bit to some bushes.

On my way back to breakfast, I wondered how long mankind would last if we didn't find a better way to wash our hands after a trip to the throne. I had a pocket full of wet naps, but they wouldn't last long. Good old lye soap and water were probably the answer to the personal hygiene issue. That made me think about sanitation in general. I didn't want to think about running out of TP. Leaves and corncobs would only make the sanitation issues much worse.

As I passed the truck, I smelled gasoline. Crap. We were in the woods, and the smell could only be coming from the truck. I walked around the truck and found the leak in the back. There was a small hole in the gas tank. I initially thought a bullet had made the hole, but it was too small. The ground was soaked with gas, so I took the truck out of gear and pushed it away from the spill. I found a small sapling and cut a small limb from it. I whittled a two-inch long plug for the hole that was tapered from about an eighth-of-an-inch up to half-inch. The plug slid in with ease. In fact, it slid too easily. The leak was where a rust spot had made a hole in the tank. The plug finally stopped sliding in, and I firmly seated it to seal the leak.

I got out from under the truck and saw Kat scratching MMax's ears. I watched her from a distance. She was good with MMax, and he liked her. That wasn't supposed to happen until I handed him to her and let him know I trusted her. I guess they'd bonded while I was with the FEMA group. I walked into camp and ate my lunch.

Kat saw me walk up. "What's that smell?"

"The truck was leaking gas. I fixed it," I said.

She asked, "Will we have enough gas to get to your home?"

"Don't know."

"You're awful quiet this morning. Do you want to talk about Ann? I know sometimes it helps to talk about what's bothering you," Kat said.

I swallowed and looked down at my food. "No, I don't need any help or a warm puppy to help me get in touch with my feelings. Ann died trying to make sure we got home safely. It's not our fault, and we will kill the jerks that killed her. It's time to move on and get to my parent's place. Let's pack up and go."

Kat stood up and saluted. "Yes, sir."

"You don't salute sergeants."

She saluted again. "Yes, sir," and then gave me the finger before she ran away to pack up her things.

I saw Kat dig into her bag. She brought out a red object that I instantly recognized, and MMax started wagging his tail and begging Kat for it. She said, "Stay," and started spooning something into the red Kong. It was peanut butter.

She held it out and said, "Good boy."

MMax went to her and gently took the Kong in his mouth. He started chewing on the Kong as he rolled around on the ground in ecstasy.

I said, "I'm glad you found a Kong for MMax, but he is trained to do something good before being rewarded with the Kong."

"MMax is always a good dog," she said.

MMax stopped and looked at me with his goofy upside down grin as if to say, "I'm always a good boy."

I rubbed his belly and decided not to spoil the moment for MMax. I would train Kat while we drove down to Walter Hill.

The gas gauge needle was barely above an eighth of a tank when we pulled back onto the road. "Kat, keep an eye out for a car or truck that we can steal some gas from. We need a garden hose to siphon the gas. Otherwise, I'll have to knock a hole in the bottom and drain the gas into a pan. That could be disastrous."

Kat said, "Stop at the next farmhouse, and we'll liberate a hose."

A few minutes later, I pulled into the driveway of a home that had an old tractor and a minivan in the driveway. I stepped out of the truck, there was a blast, and a bullet whizzed past my head. A man hid behind a tree with a rifle aimed at me.

"Get your asses offen my property before I fill you with lead!"

I said, "We just need ..."

Another blast and buckshot careened past me too darn close for comfort. "Git, now!"

I climbed back in the truck and hauled ass out of there. Kat clung to me. She said, "Well, so much for southern hospitality."

"There's no telling how many thugs tried to rob him. We need an abandoned house next time."

I knew I didn't want to go through Gallatin, so I began working my way around the southeast side of the city, cutting through suburbs and industrial parks. I saw the sign for Highway 109 and turned south at the intersection when the truck sputtered and died.

There was an old Chevy truck on the side of the road, and we coasted to a stop behind it. I looked in the bed, and there were one empty gas can and a couple of empty anti-freeze one-gallon jugs. I planned to fill these and use them to fill our truck. "Kat get all the empty cans or bottles you can find. Hand me one of those water bottles."

I cut the bottom off the water bottle and made a funnel. I had to pinch the spout down a bit to fit in the old Ford's gas tank, but it would work. "Now, I'm going to poke a hole in the tank and drain some gas out into this pan and use it to fill the gas can and these old anti-freeze jugs."

I smelled the inside of the anti-freeze jugs, and my heart sank. They had been used to store gas. I crawled under the truck and rapped on the tank only to hear the sickening sound of an empty tank. "Damn, Kat, the tank is empty. I'm going to have to walk on down the road to a house or an abandoned vehicle for more gas. I'll be back soon."

Kat picked up the two jugs. "Nope. No way, are you leaving me behind. I'm staying glued to you until we get to your home."

I frowned. "I thought you were a bad-assed-Amazon Warrior."

She rolled her eyes. "I can kill and have killed when it was necessary, but we're better off staying together. MMax, you, and I make a formidable force. I watch your back; you watch my back. MMax watches both our backs."

We walked on down the road a few blocks before we saw another vehicle that wasn't wrecked or burned. I was pleased that it was only a year or so old. That meant that it probably died with gas in its tank. "Kat, this looks promising."

I crawled under the car while Kat and MMax kept watch for danger. I could barely squeeze under it enough to get to the tank. I rapped my knife on it and heard a satisfying dull ring of a tank with gas. I moved the pan under the tank and placed the point of my knife against the bottom of the tank. I hit the butt end of my knife with my palm and only received a sharp pain for a reward.

"Kat, I need a big rock to use as a hammer. This metal is thicker than I thought."

"Yes, sir."

I chuckled but didn't say anything. Kat came back a few minutes later with a rock that would do. I hit the end of my knife, and it made a tiny hole at first. I hit it again, and my blade pierced the tank and sank in an inch. I pulled the knife out as I slide the pan under the hole. Nothing happened but a tiny drip. What the heck was wrong? Then it hit me there wasn't any way for air to get in the tank.

"Unscrew the gas cap."

Kat removed the gas cap, and a steady stream of gas poured into my pan. The half-gallon pan quickly filled, and I traded Kat for another smaller pan while she poured the gasoline into the gas can. It took fifteen minutes to fill all three containers. I stuck my knife back in the hole and had Kat screw the gas cap back on. There was a small drip, so I placed a pan under the drip.

We walked back to the truck at a fast pace and soon had the truck running. I drove down to the car to finish the job. It was tedious work, but we transferred about eight gallons into the old Ford. That should be enough to get us to my family's place, but I wanted to get more gas just in case. As I drove away, Kat yelled, "Step on it! Some men are running toward us!"

I peeled away and drove a mile before slowing up. We stopped at an industrial park and obtained a full tank for the truck from abandoned vehicles. We also filled the three containers.

Kat ran over to the side of one building and came back with ten feet of a water hose. "This should save some effort."

I patted her on the head. "Good girl."

"Good girl, my ass. If you treat me like a dog again, I'll show you what a bad girl can do."

I snickered. "Do you promise? I like bad girls."

"You are an ass. I meant I'll kick your ass if you keep messing with me," Kat said.

I couldn't take her seriously because she was only a bit larger than my right leg. I said, "I'm sorry. I promise I'll behave."

★

Chapter 11

South of Gallatin at the Cumberland River Bridge.

"Hey asshole, that's not funny. If you'd been through what I've been through, you wouldn't make that joke," Kat said as tears welled up in her eyes.

I turned her around and drew her into my chest. "I was only joking, and you are right. I don't know what you went through, and that was dumb on my part. I won't do it again."

Kat continued to sob with her face against my chest. I was only six-foot-two, but I was a giant next to her five-foot-tall figure. I hugged her and patted her on the back, promising not to be an ass ever again. I continued to hold her for a few more minutes until she pulled away and said, "Thanks for holding me until I stopped crying. Jason, I teamed up with you and MMax because I feel safe with you, and I know you wouldn't let anyone harm me. But darn it, you can be so cruel with the jokes."

I stuttered and stammered. "Again, I'm sorry for hurting you. I guess my only real experience around women has been in the Army during wartime. We always make crude jokes and pull pranks on each other. I guess I think of you as a tough woman who can dish it out as well as take it."

She stepped closer and hugged me. "Jason, I can be tough, but that one thing is off limits if you want to stay, my friend."

I lifted her face and kissed her on the forehead. "I want to be your friend and will stay away from that topic."

She stood up on her toes and kissed me on the lips. Until that moment, I had thought of her as a child because of her small size. I held her tight and returned the kiss. Then suddenly, we both pushed away. She said, "Awkward. I'm sorry for sending the wrong message."

I said, "Not a problem, but we're friends, and I want to keep it that way."

I walked away, cursing myself for my earlier joke that perhaps the thugs guarding the bridge would let us cross if she was nice to them. You know what I actually said, but now I can't even say it since I understand her pain so much more now. Let's forget what a dumbass I was back then. I promise I'm a better man now. Well, I'm trying to be better.

"Okay, Kat, starting over. What do you recommend we do to get across the bridge?"

Kat smiled her pixie like smile. "Let's list our options. We could snipe them from here. We could ram our way through their roadblock, or maybe we just swim across the river at another place and avoid the bastards."

I replied, "One is too noisy and would bring in their friends. The second will just destroy our old truck and get us killed. How well can you swim at night?"

Now, you know how I ended up swimming across the Cumberland River while towing a shrimp woman and a dog in a kid's wading pool. MMax can swim, but I didn't want him to try to swim the width of the river on his first real swim. I made both of them wear a life jacket and tied several more life jackets to the wading pool. Did I fail to mention that the lady who brought up swimming across the river can't swim a lick and is terrified of water deeper than a water glass full?

We placed our guns, clothes, and food in garbage bags to keep them dry as we waited for midnight to come. At about 1:30 am, I stripped off my clothes and stood there in my underwear. Kat made a soft whistling noise and said, "Come over here, sweetie, and I'll stick a dollar in your shorts."

I gave her the finger even though she couldn't see my hand. I walked closer to MMax, picked him up, and placed him in the wading pool. I reached out, lifted Kat, and gently placed her beside MMax. "Please stay as still as possible and try to keep MMax calm. It will take a while for me to tow the homemade raft over to the other side. Don't worry. I'm a good swimmer."

To say that things didn't go well is an understatement. Since the grid was down the river was much broader at Gallatin. The Old Hickory Locks and Dam were closed when the shit hit the fan, so now the water had to spill over the dam to continue downstream. This made the river wider. Spring rains also caused the current to flow faster. Looking back, I was foolish for trying this stunt. Things went relatively okay for the first half of the crossing even though I knew the current was washing us further downstream than planned.

I tried to keep us from going too far downstream but gave up as I tired. I concentrated on getting us to the other shore, somewhere. The flickering lights from the fires in the barrels on the bridge were long gone when I knew we were in deep crap. We must have been several miles downriver not to see the fires. We finally got close to the bank, but there wasn't a bank to land on. There were either dangerous stickups or rocky cliffs. Just when I thought I saw a place to land, a big assed log hit the wading pool and overturned it. MMax leaped into the water, and I dove to get Kat because the undercurrent took her and her lifejacket to the bottom.

After diving twice, I felt her leg hit my back and grabbed it. I wrapped my arm around her chest and rolled onto my side as I swam with one arm to the shore. Thank God, my feet hit the rocky shore, and I pulled Kat's lifeless body up on a big flat rock. I turned her on her side and let the water drain from her lungs. Then I turned her over and checked for a heartbeat. I felt a pulse, and suddenly, she spat water from her lungs and gasped for air.

Kat continued to alternate between gasping and spitting out water for a few minutes. She trembled in my arms as I tried to keep her warm. "Kat, can you talk? I need to get you to a warm place so you can recover."

She said, "Sorry."

"Sorry for what?"

"Sorry for … suggesting we swim across."

I kissed her on the forehead, picked her up in my arms, and started walking inland. I knew this was a populated area, and we should find a house quickly. Something brushed against my leg. It was MMax, and he had the end of a garbage bag with our guns and a few supplies. I hid the bag in the rocks and then felt guilty since I hadn't thought about him while trying to save Kat. "Good boy."

I patted him on the head and said, "Come on, MMax. MMax, find him."

Crap, I couldn't say, 'MMax find us a warm, cozy home,' so I hoped he would catch the scent of a man and take us to his house. As it turned out, we were only a hundred yards from a vast subdivision near the river and couldn't miss finding a house.

MMax sat and pointed in the direction we were already heading. I said, "Go," and MMax led the way to a modern cabin high on a hill overlooking the river. Carrying Kat up at least fifty steps to a huge deck wore my butt out. She was light as a feather, but even feathers get heavy after a while. The swim had sapped my strength, but I couldn't fail Kat. My legs burned, but the top of the steps was soon in sight.

The house had large windows and two sets of patio doors facing the deck and river below. I laid Kat down on a padded bench and tried both doorknobs without success. There was a small window on each end of the deck, so to keep the damage down, I chose the one on the left side. I turned the butt of my knife to the window, only to hear the awful racking sound of a 12 Gauge pump shotgun and a lady's voice.

"Put the knife and your pistol down and slowly turn around. My husband has another shotgun aimed at you, so don't try anything."

I dropped my knife and said, "MMax, watch 'em."

MMax growled as he took his on guard stance. The woman turned toward MMax, and I lunged the five feet to her, knocking her down on the deck. I rolled over the top of her and landed on my feet with the shotgun in my hands. As I hoped, there wasn't any husband or shotgun.

I said, "Lady, are you okay?"

She was mad at herself for letting me turn the tables on her. "Damn, I should have stood back further. If you're going to rob us, get it over with."

I said, "Look, my friend and I had to swim from an overturned raft, and she swallowed a lot of water. I just need to get her warm and watch her closely. She might get pneumonia, so I also have to go out and find some antibiotics."

"Why were you crossing the Cumberland at night?"

I said, "The short story is I just returned from the war over in Europe when the crap hit the fan and had to go find my sister up in Clarksville and get her home safe. We were trying to avoid the thugs who had the bridge blocked."

The woman laughed, which made me furious. "That's the truth. I don't care if you don't believe it."

The lady said, "It's probably not funny, but those are good people manning that roadblock and are trying to keep gangs and criminals from coming across the river to raid us. My husband was on duty tonight and would have let you cross."

"Oh, my God, it never dawned on me that they could be good people."

She said, "Your lady friend has been coughing ever since I saw you on the deck. She's not bringing up much, so her lungs aren't retaining a significant amount of water. I'll check her out when we get her in the house. Let's move your sister to the spare bedroom and make her comfortable. I'm not a nurse, but I've been reading survival manuals and first aid books since the lights went out."

I replied, "She's not my sister. She joined our group a while back. She is a good person who has seen bad times. My sister and her friends went on to our parent's home when we were separated by a gang up in Kentucky."

Kat woke up for a second. "Jason, where are you? Please help me."

I ran over to her and picked her up to carry her into the home. The lady said, "I'm Gwen, and I assume you're Jason. What's the girl's name?"

"She's Kat with a K. She's actually twenty-one or maybe twenty-two, and I think a part-time Country and Western singer."

Gwen said, "Take her to the last room on the right. I'll be back."

Gwen returned with several bottles of Amoxicillin and a stethoscope. She got Kat to take two of the pills. She then said, "Hold her up while I remove her shirt. A gentleman would close his eyes. Of course, if you two are a couple, you can undress her."

"My eyes are closed, and we aren't a couple."

Gwen used the stethoscope to check for Kat's breathing and to make a guess as to how much fluid remained in her lungs. "Your girlfriend is in much better shape than I could have hoped for. Now, if she can get past the next few days without a fever, she will recover quickly."

"She's not my girlfriend. I like her a lot but barely know her. She saved my dog's life, and we've saved each other's lives a few times since. Just like soldiers in a battle, you get close to people you fight side by side with," I said.

Gwen had a tear in her eye. It ran down her cheek. I asked, "Do you have a son or loved one in the service?"

"Yes, my son is in England, and my daughter is a nurse in Iceland. I don't guess I'll ever see them again."

I placed my hand on her shoulder. "Ma'am, don't be surprised if your son and daughter arrive one day on your doorstep. MMax and I were in England, we both were severely wounded and then flown to Iceland for emergency surgery. We then survived a plane crash the night the lights went out. If we can survive, your loved ones can also. Don't give up on them. Remember, No Man Left Behind."

She wiped the tears and said, "Thanks for the kind comments and giving me some hope. Let's take care of your girlfriend. Here, put these in your pocket and give her two pills every six hours until you run out of pills. We need to find some Zithromax or erythromycin. I'm going to send you out to find some medicine for your girlfriend and to help pay for her treatment."

I started to correct her again about the girlfriend comment but instead, helped her finish undressing Kat and making her comfortable. We placed several blankets over her, and Gwen quickly read up on how to treat a person who had aspirated a lot of water.

While Gwen warmed up some food for me, I couldn't help but notice there weren't any pictures of Gwen or her family on the walls or end tables. I pulled out the drawer next to me and saw a couple of picture frames. I turned them over, and there was a very distinguished couple staring back at me. They were an older gray-haired man and woman. The next picture had six men and women about the age their kids should have been. The third had all of them, plus their kids and grandchildren. Damn, this wasn't Gwen's home.

I took my soup and coffee out on the deck and dumped it over the side when she wasn't looking. MMax chewed on a Milk-Bone dog biscuit after eating a chunk of dried rabbit meat I had tossed to him. Gwen told me about her husband, Greg, and both of her children. She then looked at her watch and said, "If you don't want to get shot, we need to make sure my husband doesn't get surprised when he sees you. You stay in here, and I'll go out on the deck to greet him. I have more soup and coffee. You ate that like a starving dog."

"No thanks, I'm full," I said but wondered if it was poisoned. I knew I had to be ready for Greg when he walked in the door. I saw Gwen wave at someone as the sun began to shine through the windows. I snuck out the front door and ran around the home. I saw them talking at the top of the steps, so I cautiously climbed the steps from the garden below. Just as my head poked above the floor of the deck, I saw Greg had a shotgun and Gwen had retrieved hers.

I said, "Gwen, Greg, drop your weapons, or I'll shoot."

The man laid his shotgun on the nearest table, took Gwen's, and placed it next to his. He then pushed Gwen away from the table and said, "We don't mean you any harm and can explain the situation."

"Greg, I looked through the pictures in the drawers, and you two don't match anyone in the pictures. This isn't your home."

Gwen said, "I never said it was our home. You assumed it was our home when I caught you trying to break a window. We can explain."

I replied, "Come on in the kitchen after I pat you down."

They didn't have any weapons, so I followed them into the kitchen. Gwen said, "Let me get my purse. I'd show you photos on my cell phone, but you know I can't."

I had seen a purse on the floor next to the couch. "Go get it but no tricks. I don't want to hurt any innocent people, but I need to know who you are before trust can be solid."

Gwen retrieved the purse. I said, "Dump the contents on the table."

A pile of woman's stuff, a cell phone, and a woman's wallet fell out. She slowly opened the wallet, and a plastic folder of pictures fell out across the table. She said, "You can see Greg and me with that beautiful couple and their three children. Now, compare them to the family picture in the end table."

I compared the picture with Gwen and her husband to the one from the end table. "The young woman is your daughter, and the man is the grandson of the owner of this house."

Gwen smiled, "Yes, and this is the second time you thought we were bad people."

I asked, "This may be sensitive, but where are the rest of the people in this picture?"

Greg said, "Most live in this area and are okay. My daughter and kids are in the basement below this home. My wife sent them there until I arrive back from guard duty. See, she didn't trust you either."

I looked up and saw Kat in a mirror walking to me from behind. She walked up beside me and sat down in my lap with her arms around my neck. "Gwen, Jason is my hero. Just this week he saved a priest, two nuns, his sister, twelve women and children, and me, twice."

Gwen winked at me. "You two have been through a lot together."

"Yes, but he has an almost girlfriend down at his mom's place who has probably forgotten about him. He's a good man but kinda dense for such a great guy."

I made the time out sign with my hands, lifted Kat up, and placed her on a chair. "Look, I know I'm better at fighting wars and killing people than relationships, but dense isn't fair."

Kat saw my pistol in my lap. "Has there been a problem?"

I responded, "I failed to mention that after being shot several times, blown up by a bomb, and surviving a plane crash that I'm not a very trusting person."

Kat laughed and said, "No shit, Sherlock."

Greg and Gwen laughed. Gwen said, "Kat, Greg, are you hungry?"

Both said yes, as I raised my hand. Gwen looked perplexed then said, "You dumped your soup over the rail because you thought I was trying to poison you."

"What can I say? Kat told you I was dense."

★

Chapter 12

Northeast of Walter Hill, Tennessee.

Over five weeks had passed since Jason had left to find his sister. Zack and Jan wouldn't admit it, but they were giving up hope their son would ever return. They were pleased to have Michelle safe and back home but thought it was a cruel joke that Jason had never come back after saving his sister.

The priest's flock and Michelle had added sixteen more people to their nine already present. A week later, Zack brought a family back with him from a scavenging trip. They consisted of two brothers, one of whom had a wife and two teenaged boys. This grew the community to thirty people. Only Mark and one of the new teenage boys had to be goaded into working. All of the others were thankful for the security and safety of the compound.

Zack watched as his construction team laid the last log on the wall of their southern guard post. The four-guard posts were actually last resort defensive positions with sixteen-inch thick walls of logs. Even Father James helped with the heavy lifting. The two brothers, Ross and Rick, had worked in construction and became the leaders of most of the construction projects. They had achieved a considerable number of improvements and added ten more trailers, along with the required sanitation and water distribution infrastructure needed to support the new people.

Zack had worked on the tractor and had it humming. It had a bucket and a posthole digging attachment. Both significantly reduced the amount of labor around the growing community. Zack, Murph, Karen, and Maria raided an abandoned farm supply store and brought home a cornucopia of supplies they needed for farming, security, and construction. Murph and Maria had installed trip wires inside the several hundred yards of the fence around the compound to give early warning that intruders were close to their homes.

Zack and Jan sat in the twilight air, looking over their accomplishments. Zack was silent for a few minutes, as he smelled the honey suckle mixed with a new pungent odor. "Hon, we've been lucky so far. That whiff of foul odor is the smell of Hendersonville and Goodlettsville burning to the ground."

"Oh, my! Are you sure?"

"Yes, Murph and I traveled into Goodlettsville the other day. Several people told me there was open warfare between the two gangs. The good people are either fleeing or hiding in the rubble. So far, most people are fleeing to the south. It's only a matter of time before someone stumbles upon us."

Jan said, "Zack, you haven't mentioned Jason for several days. I didn't hear his name in your prayers last night."

"Hon, I still have hope he will return one day, but I'd be lying if I thought it was likely. Even Karen and the girls gave up on him. Murph moved into their trailer earlier this evening. Billie and Ross are getting thicker than thieves are. Our community has come together. It will thrive if we can fight off intruders for another six months.

***

"Well, did you find Sergeant Walker's family?"

"No, sir. We've searched west and south without finding them. The scum from the surrounding cities is spreading out to the countryside. The idiots have learned that burning down their cities also burned any remaining food sources. They are now looking for farms and farmers to grow food for their people."

"You bring up a good point. Our supplies won't last forever, and I don't intend to become a farmer. We need to find those farms and protect them from the bad guys. Sergeant Black, I want you to lead that effort."

"Sir, can I add a couple of the Kentucky farm boys to my team? I don't know nothing about farming."

"Take who you need. I want to add existing farms to our new security area and expand their production as quickly as possible. Be on the lookout for some agriculture professionals to help give you guidance. I'm going to concentrate on finding a secure site for our base in this area."

"Sir, what about Walker and his family?"

"We'll eventually find them. I'm not in a hurry to make him watch his loved ones die."

☆

Chapter 13

Southeast of Gallatin, Tennessee.

I was beat and fell asleep several times that morning as Kat and I got to know Gwen and Greg Johnson. Kat was still not back to full strength and needed several days to rest. I thanked the Johnsons for taking us in and promised I would go to the nearest pharmacies and stores to find more medicines, food, and ammunition.

I nodded off again, and Kat took me to our room and made me lay down for a nap. MMax lay on the bed beside me with his head pointed to the door and rested his head on my stomach as usual. MMax or I were always on guard against danger. I quickly fell asleep and slept through the evening until early morning, when I heard the door squeak a bit. MMax gave a low growl and then laid his head back down. I saw Gwen looking in at me.

"So, she's not your girlfriend. Someone had better tell her," Gwen said as she chuckled and left.

I didn't know when Kat had crawled into bed with me, but my arm was around her. We had all our clothes on so get your dirty mind out of the gutter. She was sound asleep, and I didn't want to wake her, so I tried to sleep until daylight. That didn't work, so I planned the search for supplies and then moved on to planning our trip home. MMax whimpered his, 'Get up Jason, I got to pee,' whimper. I pushed him off the bed and unwrapped myself from Kat. She woke just enough to say, "Thanks for holding me last night. I was scared and needed you."

"Kat, thanks for holding me last night. I need a friend."

She made a huffing sound, and I heard, "Geez Louise, what does a girl have to do?"

I swatted her on the butt and said, "Be patient. Remember I'm dense."

After a full day of meeting Gwen and Greg's relatives and friends, we ate a full meal and stayed up swapping 'Where we were when the lights went out stories.' One of Greg's friends went before me and said, "I was going down the road at sixty miles per hour and ran off the road when the engine died. Imagine being the unlucky sucker who was in an airplane."

Kat and Gwen laughed at what he'd said; this made him a bit perturbed. Greg waved his hand and said, "Jason, tell them where you were when the shit hit the fan."

I stood up and spoke. "I had been wounded in Europe in an IED explosion and was on a medivac plane flying home to Nashville when the EMP bombs killed the plane's engines and electronics. The plane crashed. The crew and most of my Army friends were killed in the crash. Our medical pods saved MMax and me."

I sat down to complete silence. The man said, "You win for having the worst situation I can imagine."

I said, "No. The people in the house where our plane hit and destroyed had the worst situation. They were burned alive. I just hope I'm wrong and the impact killed them."

I swallowed the last sip from my fourth glass of homemade wine and excused myself. I started down the hall with MMax and Kat following. "Kat, you can stay up and enjoy the company."

She replied, "I'm tired and tired of the conversation. I don't want to think back to the early days. It scares me."

We entered our room, and I placed some lawn chair cushions on the floor for MMax and me to sleep on. Kat peeled her clothes off and stood there. She said, "Come on and sleep in the bed with me. I feel safer cuddled up to you. Please."

I guess I still had a thing for Karen so as much as my body said yes, I said, "Kat, that sounds inviting, but I can't sleep with anyone in my bed due to PTSD. I might wake up and strangle you."

Of course, I made that up, and she didn't believe me because every time I woke up, Kat was glued to me. She must have had some horrible nightmares because she cried in her sleep, and one time, she beat on my back and said, "No. No. Stop."

I held her close, and she went back to sleep. Several times, I picked her up and placed her in her bed, only to find her again on the floor with me in the morning. Most nights, MMax was the only one sleeping in the bed. I didn't want her to get too close to me because I was too messed up for a woman to depend on me.

I wasn't a mean or bad man to women. Just the opposite was true. I had great respect for women and fell for them too quickly. I was also afraid of commitment, so Maria and our 'friends with benefits' was the perfect situation for me.

MMax ran out and down the back steps to the river and found his way to our bags with our weapons and supplies. He brought them one at a time, back up the long stairs to the top of the deck. He smelled some evil men, but they were far away. He stayed on the deck for an hour, but the smell didn't get stronger, so he scratched on the door, and Gwen opened it. MMax went inside and joined Jason.

***

Benders Ferry Road was pretty much deserted in the hours before the sun rose that morning. We had two old farm wagons pulled by one horse each. The air was crisp and clean close to the river. The closer we were to Mt. Juliet, foul odors wafted on the breeze. There were buildings smoldering and open sewage dumped by the roadside. The smell was stifling. MMax didn't seem to mind the scent, but he was known to wallow in piles of cat crap from time to time. He always thought he was being punished when I washed him after he'd spent so much effort.

Kat had pitched a bitch of a fit when I told her she had to stay and rest. It had been over a week since we'd nearly drowned and she was raring to get back to normal. I promised her she could go on the next scrounging foray. She still bitched and moaned and groaned but did what I told her to do. She was a very hardheaded and stubborn young lady.

I took the point with MMax on guard for the usual dangers. Several dogs barked a ways off, and an occasional cat cried out in the dark, but it was otherwise quiet until we arrived at the outskirts of the city. MMax growled, and a small dog ran towards us from between two abandoned cars. I almost shot the Shih Tzu, but MMax blocked my aim by stepping between us to greet the dog. They suddenly turned toward the cars, and several Coyotes pounced from the darkness. MMax bit one dog, shook him, and pitched the body down the street. The Shih Tzu tackled one but only succeeded in backing that one down until MMax could dispatch it. I took my hatchet and cleared the remaining two away. Greg kicked another, and they high tailed it back into the woods.

I asked, "Is everyone okay?"

Greg replied, "I'm okay. The others didn't make contact. Is MMax okay?"

I took MMax behind the wagon and used my small flashlight to check him out. I couldn't find any wounds. This made me conscious that neither MMax nor I were equipped as well as we normally were in battle. I needed to make him a vest out of canvas or leather that would protect him from bites and thorns.

Our goal was a strip mall on the north end of Mt. Juliet. There were several retail stores, a CVS Pharmacy, a Kroger, and a sporting goods store. We realized they had probably been ransacked by locals and drug addicts but hoped they'd overlooked a few things. I staged everyone behind the CVS and said, "Greg, take the lead at the Kroger. Paul will take over when we get to the CVS, since you know medicines the best, and I'll take the animal shelter and the Animal Hospital next door."

Paul was impatient and didn't like taking orders. "Yeah, yeah, boss, man."

Greg got in his face. "Sergeant Walker has experience at this. You don't. Get with the program."

Paul was an emergency room doctor who thought he was better than the rest of us and a bit lazy. He was Greg's ex-son-in-law. He was a pompous ass, and Greg's daughter had gotten tired of his condescending demeanor and skirt-chasing. She'd taken him to the cleaners, and he hated Greg because Greg had hired the high priced lawyer who stuck it to Paul. Paul replied, "Yes, Daddy dearest. Whatever."

I said, "Paul, the medicines will be a mess. Don't be afraid to scoop pills off the floor and look everywhere. Addicts will destroy the place to find narcotics. Everyone, remember we shouldn't overlook abandoned, private homes, businesses, and factories after our initial targets. I want us back on the road by 9:00 am sharp. Stay together,

MMax and I'll be the lookouts for the first two, and Greg and John will watch our backs while we search the Animal Hospital. Let's go."

The grocery store was picked clean. Sadly, several bodies were strewn around the store and were half-eaten and all rotten. The smell would gag a maggot. We did find a fully stocked first aid kit by the manager's office. Greg also found a few cans of tuna and soup in the employees' lockers. The employee vending machine was lying upside down on the floor, stripped clean. We moved on to the CVS Pharmacy.

Paul was actually helpful and worked hard searching for medicines. As I'd expected, the over the counter medicines and pharmacy looked like a bomb had devastated the place. Pill bottles had been thrown against the walls with pills scattered everywhere. Paul made everyone find a broom and dustpan, and we swept up the pills and placed them in plastic bags.

I heard Paul yell with glee, "I found one!"

I looked into the front doorway and asked, "What did you find?"

"I found two more! Those are pill identification books. They tell nurses and doctors what each pill is used for and what it looks like. These for prescription drugs, and that one is for over the counter drugs. We need some more, if possible, to help sort this mess of pills."

I said, "I guess the police also used them to spot narcotics."

The man looked at me in a weird way. "I guess so."

Greg later told me that Paul had abused drugs in the past, and that was why the weird look.

We found bags full of toilet paper, paper towels, feminine hygiene products, and household cleaners. We loaded up one whole wagon, just from the CVS store.

The animal shelter wasn't as bad as I feared. There was a crude note on the door that read, "We released all of the animals. We couldn't care for them anymore. May God smile kindly on them."

I hate to admit it, but Paul actually knew which animal drugs were equivalent to human medicines. I knew a few, but he was a big help. The obvious narcotics were all gone, but as before the antibiotics and run of the mill medicines were thrown about haphazardly. Most were still in their plastic bottles. We quickly gathered every pill, bandage, and veterinarian medical device. Many could be used on humans.

The animal shelter was much the same, nothing but generic type pain medicines but nothing to get high on. I opened a back office and found an older man and a half-naked young girl. The man had been shot in the head, and the teenaged girl had been violently raped before being shot several times. I became sick to my stomach when I realized the girl could have been my sister or Kat and slammed the door shut. I just made a slashing motion across my throat and walked away.

We were finished early and ready to go when MMax growled and pointed to a building across the street. "Take cover and have your weapons ready. MMax, search for man."

MMax led me across the street, but I made sure we kept stalled cars between the building and ourselves. We left the safety of cover provided by a van and worked our way around an adjacent building to come out behind the target building. As expected, there were several dirty looking people passing a bottle around trying to work up the courage to attack my friends across the street. The idiots had clubs, knives, and two pistols. I drew my knife and a hatchet I'd found at Greg's place.

Clearing my throat got their attention. One man stepped out front, "Mister, those drugs and food are ours. We own this block. Give them up or die."

The fool slurred his words, so I knew he was high or drunk. I felt terrible about what happened next. I threw my knife and yelled, "MMax attack!" My knife sliced into the man's chest. He stared at me, dropped his pistol, and fell to the ground. MMax bit the man's arm with the gun while I backed the others off with my pistol. I said, "MMax, hold'em!"

MMax bit with more pressure and the man burst into tears begging me to call my dog off. "MMax, Out!" MMax let the man go. "MMax, watch 'em!"

MMax released his bite and stayed ready to attack again. I said, "I should shoot all of you now. If I see you here again, I will personally kill every last one of you."

One of the men ran at me with his baseball bat. I blocked the bat with my hatchet, sidestepped, and sliced his back open with the razor sharp hatchet blade. The man whimpered as he bled out. "Anyone else feel lucky? I've killed a thousand men and women in Europe and won't blink an eye killing scum like you."

One man had a puddle by his shoe as he pissed himself. They heard what I said and ran as if their asses were on fire. I laughed at them and then turned to face a new danger as MMax growled behind me. The men who had come with me were standing behind me and had apparently seen most of the action. Their faces were pale.

Paul was the only one red in the face. "Did you have to kill them?"

I shook my head and said, "No, I probably should have let them kill you and keep raping and killing people for drugs. It was just your lucky day, and I felt like killing someone."

Paul said something under his breath and headed to the wagons. I looked at the others and said, "I was only kidding, Paul. I only killed a few hundred in Europe and killed these two to make the point that they would die if they messed with your group. I'm leaving soon, and I don't think most of you have the guts to defend yourselves. I want you to survive and thrive, but I have my doubts."

Greg motioned for the others to listen. "We don't have your experience, but except for Paul, these men and a few women will do what it takes to protect our homes and supplies."

"I hope you are right. Let's go home. It's daylight, and this will expose us to anyone with a gun along the way. Have the team place the tarps over the supplies and let's roll home."

Okay, I can be a bit intense, but I know when it's needed and when to be cool. Greg and crew needed my little show, even though I didn't plan it to happen. I learned on the way home, I was wrong about these men and their resolve.

We were ambushed twice on the way home. One attack was by another bunch of druggies who couldn't shoot straight and didn't know the difference between concealment and cover. The dumbasses hid behind a row of bushes and shot at us. Greg and several of the men unleashed a wall of double ought buckshot into the bushes from twenty-five feet, and four drugged out jerks died.

The next problem was a roadblock a mile before we arrived home. The idiots had placed the barrier so it could be seen a half a mile away. I sent a team to flank them while I snuck in closer with my pistol. The guys came upon the three men who planned to rob us and shot them dead where they stood. I didn't fire a shot.

I gave them a thumbs-up, and we rejoined the others for a peaceful rest of the way to Greg's home. Kat and the other women ran out to greet us. Kat hugged me and told me she was glad I had returned safely. It was only noon, and we'd had a full day. Gwen fixed a late breakfast for us. I ate and went to our room to catch some rack time. I laid on the bed, trying to sleep when Kat slid in beside me.

She said, "Don't try to run me off. I'll just make you miserable until you give up."

"Kat, I'm afraid that you will get too close, and I'll hurt you. Please let me sleep on the floor if you stay in the room," I said.

Kat pulled my face close to hers. "Hey, you got this wrong. I don't want you that way. I'm just afraid to close my eyes, and you're comfortable like a big brother. Just think of me as your sister."

I choked a bit but said, "That will work, but you have to stop running around the room half naked."

Then it took me an hour to clear all the non-brotherly thoughts about Kat from my mind. That was tough with me spooned up to her back. I went to sleep saying, *"Sister, sister, sister,"*… to myself.

I rolled over when I heard her snoring and slept until Gwen woke us up. Kat was plastered to my back, and MMax was beside her. Gwen said, "Would you and Kat like to join us for supper?"

She winked at me and left the room.

I know Gwen thought we were doing more than sleeping. I knew I had to actually treat Kat like a brother would, and that didn't include spooning against each other all night.

★

Chapter 14

Southeast of Gallatin, Tennessee.

While Kat took her turn tending the garden, I had a straightforward conversation with Gwen and Greg. I didn't have much time, so I dove in quickly.

"Both of you have asked Kat and me to stay with you and become part of the group. I have to go home to my parents and sister, but could Kat stay with you?"

Gwen's eyebrows wrinkled. "Did you two break up? I hope not."

I said, "Ma'am, I've been trying to tell you that we aren't a couple. Of course, I care for Kat, and under different circumstances, we would have been more than friends. She needs a safe environment, as much as is possible these days. My parents would welcome her, but

I'm not the guy for her. I'm not ready for a relationship and don't want to hurt her."

Gwen said, "You could have fooled me. You two sleep together."

"Yes, we sleep in the same room. We have never …uh …you know."

Gwen laughed. "You are a grown man. You can say the word sex."

This was just like talking about sex to my mom. "Yes, and we never had …sex."

Greg said, "Jason, it will break her heart. She adores you."

This was going south quickly. "Will it go any better if Kat finally realizes I don't care for her the way she wants me to after we arrive at my family and friend's compound? She was so hurt but sweet and nice when I met her. I never could have hurt her more by misleading her if we became intimate. I tried my best to comfort her and make her feel safe to get over the pain from being attacked months ago."

Gwen had a frown, and a tear dribbled down her cheek. "We didn't know she'd been attacked. Oh, crap, you're right. Better, she's hurt and stays with us than busting her bubble among people she wants to escape from after she's hurt. When do you plan to break it to her and leave?"

"I plan to tell her tonight and leave in the morning. She's a hard person to say no to, but I don't want to sneak away without telling her first."

Southeast of Lebanon, Tennessee.

The next day, we left the Johnson's home, sharing a ride on the only horse they could spare. Kat was behind me with her arms around my waist. We took Burton Road over to Highway 109 South on the way to my folks home. Kat tried to speak with me several times, but I was still pissed that she had ignored everything I'd said about not loving her and about staying with the Johnsons.

I continued to ignore her until I heard. "Jason, you don't listen to a thing I say. I've told you a hundred times that I'm not interested in you, other than I feel safe around you, and I do like you but not that way."

I grinned because a thought entered my worn out mind. "Okay, you can come on to my folk's home, but you have to sleep in another room. I don't want you hanging on when Maria and I hook back up."

She gritted her teeth but forced herself to smile. "Who's Maria?"

"I've told you about Maria. She was in my unit in Europe and was my 'friends with benefits' lady. I can't have you clinging to me when my girlfriend joins us."

I could feel the blast of hot air expelled from her lips as I heard, "Hunnnh," and felt her arms loosen around my waist.

Oops. Oh, sorry. I failed to mention earlier that Kat ignored everything I'd said and came with me to my parents. She didn't pitch a hissy fit or scream. She just said, "I'm going with you. You can let me join you, or I'll follow you. The outcome will be the same. Let's go."

I can still remember those days, and I still think she was the most stubborn woman I had ever met. She says strong willed. I say, stubborn like a mule.

Kat stopped the jabbering, and I could think again. I'm a dumbass. I should have flaunted Maria to her much earlier. I believe somehow 'Bad Jason' might have been interested in Kat, but 'Good Jason' won the battle. I know talking about yourself in the third person sounds a bit nuts but excuse me, because this was a very trying time in my life. Dealing with nutty, clinging women, killing bad guys, and trying to survive were about all I could handle.

Enough about my problems, now back to the story.

The Johnson's home on the river was only twenty-six miles from my parent's place. I didn't want someone stealing our only horse, so we only traveled at night. Horses shod with metal horseshoes make a racket, and you can actually see sparks on the pavement. To reduce the noise and help the poor horses, we traveled on dirt roads or the side of the highways, which slowed us down quite a bit.

We stopped for the night, only about eight miles from the Johnson's place southwest of Highway 109, and 40 junctions. There were several abandoned quarries, and we rode to the high side of one, so no one could sneak up on us from the rear. The front side had a clear view of about a hundred yards. We lucked out, and there was a huge quarry truck parked facing Highway 109 in the distance. MMax growled a couple of times during the night; it was a pack of coyotes howling nearby the quarry.

Throwing Maria in Kat's face had worked. Kat curled up on the seat as far from me as she could get. It was a chilly night, and I missed the warmth from her body. The dirty traitor MMax curled up against Kat. What the heck was that about? MMax was my best friend. Later that night, I felt the seat shake a bit and realized she was sobbing. I wanted to comfort her but knew cutting it off now was for her own good.

Earlier I said, 'Dealing with nutty clinging women, killing bad guys, and trying to survive were about all I could handle.' Well, the next day, how much I could handle was severely tested. I woke up and found myself alone in the big quarry truck. MMax had left to keep Kat company. Bad dog. I needed to have a heart to heart talk with my dog before Kat totally stole him from me.

I searched the area and neither Kat nor MMax were found. I wasn't worried about MMax, but there were too many less than honorable men trying to survive who would love to get their hands on Kat. I checked my weapons and left the rest of my gear in the cab of the truck. The horse was hobbled and only a few yards from where it started last night. The grass was thick, and there was a puddle of water from the rain a couple of days ago.

I found their tracks by walking in a circle around the front of the truck and followed them into a stand of trees toward the highway. They were easy to follow because they cut two swaths through the lush, green grass. I broke through a group of brushes to see Kat on her knees with MMax beside her. They were a dozen feet or so from an improvised shack. She faced away from me, so I couldn't see what she was doing. I was about ten feet from her when I heard her crying. Then I saw some small feet sticking out on her right side.

I didn't want to scare her, so I softly said, "Kat, are you okay?"

She didn't flinch or move, but MMax turned to look at me. He didn't even wag his tail. I raised my voice a bit, "Kat! Are you …?"

She whirled around with a knife in hand and sprang to her feet, ready to fight. There was rage in her red, watery eyes. She saw me and dropped the knife. "Someone cut their heads off."

Kat buried her head in my chest and cried as I looked at the three small, headless bodies. Tears washed down my cheeks, and my mind couldn't wrap itself around what kind of monster could do this. The children had been killed recently and had fresh bites that probably were from the pack of coyotes we heard last night.

I drew my gun. "Kat, please stay over here while I check out the shack. MMax, search for man!"

***

MMax instantly knew the smell of the evil man who had gotten away months ago. MMax didn't know fear but had a tingling feeling that ran from his neck to his tail. He wanted to kill the man before he killed again. MMax sniffed the air and could tell the scent was a day old. MMax heard a sound behind him but remained focused on sniffing the air for the evil man's scent.

***

I saw MMax sit facing north without moving. This confused me because MMax always did what I told him to do. I repeated the search commands and pointed to the shack. MMax went into the hut ahead of me, and the horror continued inside. There were a headless, naked woman and the lower torso of a man. I walked out of the shack, leaned against a tree and upchucked until my stomach was empty and the taste of bile sickened me. I wiped my mouth and said, "Don't go in there. I'll take the kid's bodies inside, and we'll burn the shack to keep them from being eaten. We need to get the hell out of here before these monsters return."

Kat held me tight as we rode south several hundred feet west of Highway 109 in our haste to get away from whatever or whoever had killed that family. There were plenty of trees and bushes to hide us from the highway on our left and scattered houses on our right

178

side. Kat didn't speak for several hours. She just clung to me and sobbed the whole way. We had traveled about four miles before I steered our horse into a clump of bushes behind a warehouse. I helped Kat to the ground and then gave her a Cliff Bar and a bottle of water from my saddlebag. She pushed the Cliff Bar away.

"Kat, we missed breakfast. You need to eat."

She moaned, "I can't, my stomach is still queasy."

I took a bite from a Nature Valley bar and stuck it in her face. She bit a small piece off and took my water from my hand. She chugged some water down and stole the rest of my bar. She washed the bar down and said, "Who could do something like that?"

"I don't know, but I'll kill them if I get a chance."

She said, "I'll help you kill them. I'll neuter the bastards."

I put my arms out. "Come here. I need a hug."

"You said that you didn't like me."

Shaking my head, I said, "No, I said I didn't love you. I like you a lot and if things were different ..."

Oh, shit, I gave her hope.

She wrapped her arms around me and didn't let go for a few minutes. I released my arms and moved to the horse. I motioned for her to join me, and we were quickly on the way south again. This time, she wouldn't stop talking. I thought about tossing out how much I wanted to see Maria again but didn't want to make Kat start crying again.

The picture of three dead headless kids haunted me for the rest of my life. The only good that came from that horrible day was I could now kill horrible men and women without remorse. The only thing that bothered me more was that we were only ten miles from my folk's home.

The small group of buildings had been an old strip mall back in the day. The sign in front said, "Antique and Flea Market." There were tables in front of each storefront, so the owners could display their wares. Kat pointed to the buildings. "Can we stop here for a few minutes? My butt is sore, and they might have something we need."

"Good idea, but make it quick. I want to make tracks to my home."

She walked to the first building, pulled something from her pocket, and worked on the door for a minute. The door opened, and she motioned for me to join her. The sign on the door said, "Books, old tools, and other manly stuff."

"How did you open the door? You're pretty resourceful for a girl."

"You could have left off resourceful. I learned that trick from a friend when we broke into Dad's liquor room."

"Your dad had a room just for liquor?"

"Yes, and he had a wine cellar and a walk-in cooler for his fancy beer."

The tiny light came on in my brain. "Your parents were rich, weren't they?"

Kat almost looked ashamed of her parents. "Yes, we were filthy rich, and I didn't appreciate the money or advantages. I was a spoiled, rich bitch who had sports cars, unlimited credit cards, and worthless friends. This damned end of the world shit forced me to grow up. You wouldn't have liked me a year ago."

Kat headed to the books, and I walked to the manly stuff. The shop was clean and well organized. Apparently, no one was interested in antiques for their survival. The old wrenches, power tools, and chains didn't catch my eye, but the antique woodworking tools did. I picked up a hand drill that was the old brace and bit holder. It had the big wooden knob and crank to turn the bit through wood. I exclaimed, "Damn, this will still drill through wood and steel if you have plenty of time."

I sorted through the wares and selected a couple more drills, two handsaws, planes, and a device to make round pegs. I saw several coffee cans full of nails and took them. There were several old duffel bags and canvas tool bags hanging on the wall. I took one of each, stuffed the tools in the bags, and then tied them to the saddle. I returned in time for Kat to yell, "Look at these books on how to make stuff the old fashioned way!"

She poked a book under my nose, and sure enough, there were detailed instructions on how to use antique woodworking tools. I thumbed through them and said, "Kat, you done good. This will be a great help to our group."

"Will you be able to build our own home when we get to your dad's place?"

"Kat, you never give up, do you?"

She smiled and said, "Not when I set my mind on something."

Crap, the Maria comments had worn off. I felt I needed to push her away without being cruel. I wanted

182

to think that through before sticking my foot in my mouth or hurting her.

I used the book as a shopping list and added awls, wood chisels, files, and a hand powered grinder to sharpen a few of the tools.

We searched the rest of the shops but didn't find anything light enough to carry home. I made a mental note to scavenge some flea markets and antique stores when we got home.

I helped Kat on the horse and got on behind her this time, for a different ride to help our sore butts. Neither of us had ridden much in our lives, and we were both saddle sore. It was a dumb and wrong move. I ended up with one arm around her waist and put a smile on her face. I started humming an old Brooks and Dunn song, *My Maria*. When I got to the part where they sing, "I love you," she pushed my arm away and muttered something under her breath.

★

Chapter 15

Several miles north of the Walker farm.

The two small children ran out of the woods and onto the dirt road. They were nearly trampled by our horse before he could stop. Kat and I started to pick the kids up when one yelled, "Dogs!"

With all the commotion, I didn't hear MMax growling and barking. What took place next, played out in front of me in slow motion. Reflexes took over for MMax and me. Several dogs charged out of the woods, and MMax jumped on the first one. The dogs tumbled across the road with MMax's jaws clamped to the other's neck. MMax's quick action gave me the extra second I needed to draw and shoot the next two dogs. The gunfire scared the others away. They ran back into the woods as quickly as they had arrived. I turned to see the other dog was dead from a massive gash on his neck and MMax licking the blood from his muzzle.

The smell of the burnt gunpowder and blood filled my nostrils as I turned to see if Kat was okay. MMax was by her side as smoke swirled in a lazy, upward spiral from her pistol. She was speechless and in a stupor. I pulled her to my chest and soothed her down while she trembled in my arms. I felt closer to her than ever and hated myself for not backing away from her. That would have pissed her off and demonstrated that I didn't care for her. I was deep in thought when the children's' crying shook me back to reality.

The little boy sobbed, and his sister tried to calm him. She was only about five-years-old but finally got him to stop crying. Kat broke free from our embrace. She picked up the little boy and said, "Whew, I think his diaper needs changing. Where are your parents?"

MMax growled, and I heard the bushes rustle deep in the woods. People's voices could be heard as they ran toward us. "Kat, take the kids behind that abandoned car."

I took cover behind a tree and waited for the gunfight to start. Then I heard a woman's voice. "Jenny, Mikey, yell if you hear me!"

I took a chance and yelled, "Your kids are safe! They're over here!"

Two men charged out of the woods with pistols in their hands. "Give us our kids!"

I said, "Lower your pistols, or you're going to die."

They hadn't seen me yet, but the men knew I had the drop on them. Then they heard Kat say, "We have you in a crossfire. If the kids are yours, they will run to you."

A woman stepped out of the woods and said, "Please let Jenny and Mikey come to me."

The girl yelled, "Mommy, Mommy, they saved us from the dogs! Don't hurt them!"

The kids ran to the woman, and the men dropped their guns. I had Kat pick up their weapons and said, "You, the one with the John Deere hat. You look familiar. Don't you own a farm just down the road a piece?"

"Yes, but sorry, I don't recognize you. I'm Jim Thorn, and that's my son and daughter-in-law. The kids you saved from that damned pack of dogs are my grandchildren. I guess we owe you for saving them."

I replied, "I'm Jason Walker, and my dad and mom own a small farm about three miles down the road and a mile or so east."

"Hell, it's a small world. I've known Zack and Jan for years. You must be the son who joined the army."

"Yes, I got back from Europe the day the grid went down. How are things around here? I came home a month ago but left quickly to go find my sister."

"It's getting better in some areas but worse in others. You can't trust anyone now. People are hungry and steal to feed their families. Our gardens are coming in now, and strangers are raiding farms as they walk through heading south. I hate it, but we've had to scare them away and even had to shoot a few. Hunger is a mighty, strong force."

I said, "It's not much better north of here. FEMA forced farmers to give up their farms and work on government farms to feed people in the larger cities. The leader was corrupt and running the camp like his own empire. Hey, Kat, give them their guns."

The man hesitated and then spoke. "That sounds like the rumors I've heard about a group of ex-Army people taking over Murfreesboro and the farms close to the city. They say they will protect farmers from the thugs and strangers but want a large cut of the crops in payment. We don't want any part of General Long's empire."

I did a double-take. "Did you say, General Long?"

"Yes, do you know him?"

I was sure the Long I knew was dead. "No, I don't think so. The Long I knew was a captain, and I'm sure he was killed a month back. If he lived, he would look like a monster with a crushed face."

The man looked shocked. "That sounds like him. How well did you know him?"

I saw my new friend fingering his pistol. "Well enough to help kill him. He worked for the general who helped FEMA subjugate the farmers north of here. I was sure he was dead. Now, I'm not sure. Let me get my dad up here to meet with you in a few days. It doesn't matter who the man is. He still has to be stopped."

The man's hand moved from his gun, and he said, "I'm looking forward to seeing Zack again."

***

The Walker farm northeast of Walter Hill Tennessee

The rise was just high enough to give him a good view of the Walker farm. It was far enough away that no one would notice him spying on them. He had to throw a poncho on the ground since it had rained last night. He waited for one of the women or young girls to stray away by themselves, so he could take one for himself. These people were well disciplined and always traveled in pairs. Usually, a man accompanied every female, and except for the priest, all were armed.

He had just about given up on them several days ago when he saw the boy. The same brat had come to his grandparent's home with that woman. He wanted that woman and dreamed about what he would do to her after he had her and killed the brat in front of her. She had embarrassed him so much in front of his grandma and grandpa that he'd went crazy and killed both of them.

Billie Johnson had to die after he had his fill of her.

Ray saw the Springer Spaniel sniffing the air and turn toward him. He knew he only had a few minutes to leave or confront several of the armed farmers. He quickly slid back into the woods and left the area. He needed some more toys to play with. That family north of Gladesville had died too suddenly. Their heads hung from the ceiling of his new home. It was an old cabin in the woods about five miles north of where Billie and her son Mark lived.

***

The air was clean but a bit humid due to last night's rain. MMax led the way as usual and became somewhat excited as he caught faint whiffs of familiar odors. He smelled the older good woman, the woman and her daughters, and the man his Jason smelled like. He also smelled a couple of new people that he didn't know. None smelled with the stench of evilness, so he ignored them. Then he caught the smell of Father James and was happy.

MMax turned to Jason with his tail wagging and barked. He pranced around, happy to be back with Jason's family. The wind shifted, and MMax changed his demeanor, stood rigid pointing northeast, and growled. This wasn't his low warning growl. It was his about to bite your ass growl.

***

"Your dog is so unpredictable," Kat said.

"Hold on, Kat," I said as I slid off the horse and helped her down. I led the horse into a stand of trees and watched for whatever or whoever had spooked MMax. I said, "MMax doesn't spook easily. Something or someone is watching us from afar. MMax caught his scent."

Kat hid behind me with that huge .50 caliber pistol drawn. A noise came from the woods close by, and she wrapped one arm around me and poked the gun out by my side.

I laughed when a rabbit bounded by. "Don't pull the trigger. The blast will fry our eyebrows and blow out our eardrums. Besides, don't you only have a few bullets left?"

"Shut up. I was startled and grabbed for my 9mm but brought out the Desert Eagle. We need to find some ammo for it. Hey, you changed the subject. Do you think MMax caught wind of that monster that killed those people?"

"He caught wind of something bad. If I took him off the leash, he'd probably go attack it, or maybe him. MMax hates whatever it is. I've wondered if it's the same man who tried to molest Billie."

"Kat tucked the hog leg back into her waistband. "Aren't we close to your home?"

I smiled. "Yep, it's only about a half a mile that way."

We were a bit more careful as we walked closer to my home after that rabbit scare. The driveway to the house was just down about fifty yards, and the driveway was about a hundred yards on to the home. MMax stopped and pointed into the woods. We heard a man's and then a woman's voice. I didn't want to eavesdrop, but these could be bad people. I motioned Kat to follow me into the bushes. Oh crap! Two naked people were doing what naked people do, in the woods on a blanket. I couldn't see the woman's face at first. I placed my hand over Kat's eyes, and she promptly slapped it away. The man moved, and holy shit! It was my Maria staring me in the eyes, naked as a jaybird. I pushed Kat back and heard. "Jason, you're alive!"

Kat was confused at first but stopped me from pushing her through the bushes and said, "Oh, my God, that was the Maria you were so hot to get back to, and she's doing a guy in the woods."

I grabbed her arm and rushed her back to the horse. I wanted to be far away before they could get their clothes on. The funny thing was that I wasn't a bit jealous. Kat hummed the Brooks and Dunn 'My Maria' tune for a minute and then never teased me about Maria again, but she held me even closer as we turned down the driveway to my parent's home.

A man I didn't know challenged us with a shotgun aimed at our bellies. Then I heard, "Stop! It's Jason! Let them come on in."

The man said, "But Zack said to disarm any visitors."

Billie replied, "You're just lucky he didn't take that shotgun and ram it where the sun don't …"

Billie stuttered as she saw Kat clinging to me. "Jason, I see you have picked up a new friend."

I turned my horse, so Kat and Billie could meet. "Billie, this is Kat. Kat, Billie and her son are the two I told you about. You know, the ones I ran over in my cart the day after the shit hit the fan. Kat and I have saved each other's lives many times. I …uh…"

I stopped in mid-sentence when I saw Karen walking hand in hand with my friend Murph in the distance. I saw them kiss and my blood boiled. Billie saw them and yelled, "Karen! Murph! Jason's back, and he brought …!"

Kat interrupted her, "His girlfriend Kat."

Billie looked puzzled. Kat replied, "Jason brought me, his girlfriend back with him."

Kat kissed me on the cheek and hugged me. I didn't understand at first, then played along. "I'm sorry; Kat and I hooked up a while back. I can't wait for her to meet Mom and Dad."

I slid off the horse, helped Kat to the ground, and kissed her in front of the growing crowd. I said, "This is Kat and MMax, and I owe our lives to her. I'm glad to see all of you but need to see my …"

Michelle nearly knocked me off my feet when she jumped in my arms. I saw a look that could kill from Kat. I said, "Michelle, I'm so glad you made it safely home. Kat, this is my sister, Michelle. Michelle, this is my girl, Kat."

Kat's frown turned into a grin as Michelle hugged me tightly. I saw my mom and dad running to us. Mom yelled, "My boy's home! Jason some thought you were dead! I never gave up hope!"

While all of this was going on, MMax saw Tina run up and sit beside Missy. MMax began whimpering and begging to go to see Tina. I said, "Go," and MMax and Tina ran off to play.

Kat said, "Well, MMax didn't introduce us to his mate."

I jerked my head toward Kat. "What?"

Kat said, "I guess they need some alone time."

That was too much info for me. I had enough trouble with women and didn't need to delve into my dog's love life.

My mom and dad hugged me for a few minutes, and then I introduced Kat. Mom hugged her and led her to the house with Dad and me following. I noticed Karen looking on but didn't say anything to her. I whispered to Dad. "I noticed several folks thought I was dead. Oh, tell your guards to keep their clothes on and eyes alert, and no one will sneak up on them and embarrass them."

Dad said, "Damn it. I would have thought Maria and Pete could keep it in their pants long enough to help keep us alive."

"Dad, well to be honest. Maria and I …"

"Son, that's TMI. Now, tell me about this young lady you brought back home. You left pining for Karen and come back with this girl."

"Dad, it's a long story. Give us time to settle in and, I'll catch you up on Kat and me, and you can tell me about Maria and this guy Pete and Karen and Murph."

Just before we stepped on the deck, Missy and Chrissy hit me from both sides. "Jason, we knew you weren't dead. We told Mom to wait. Jason …"

I hugged both girls and said, "This is Kat, my girlfriend. Kat, these beautiful young women are Missy and Chrissy. They belong to my friend Karen. I told you about them."

Kat gave each a hug as they looked at her with a confused look on their faces. "I'll see y'all later. I need some time with my mom and dad. Mom, can Kat and I have my old room?"

I knew Mom wouldn't be wild about unmarried people sharing a room in her house and secretly hoped she would separate us. Mom looked at Dad. "Sure, Jason, your room is just as you left it. I'll add some extra towels, and I think I have some clothes that will fit Kat."

I closed the door behind me after I followed Kat into my room. I took Kat by the shoulder and turned her around to face me. I kissed her on the cheek. "Kat, thanks for saving my dignity. Both women I thought wanted me, obviously didn't like me enough to wait for me. I guess I was full of myself and …"

Kat said, "Stop. Jason, you're a great guy, and any woman would love to be yours. I do. I know you don't care for me like I do for you, but I'm willing to play along to … Damn, I don't know what I'm doing, but I don't want you to show them they hurt you."

"I do care for you, Kat. It's just that I might care for you too much. I'm only used to one night stands and friends with benefits. You are special and deserve to be treated special. I don't know if I'm able to do that," I said as I watched her eyes water.

I pulled her close and hugged her for a while. "Kat, I don't want any other woman in my life. I'm just not ready to be what you need."

I kissed her on the top of the head, picked her up, and laid her on the bed. I sat in the rocker next to the bed and tried in vain to sleep.

Later, Mom poked her head in and thought we were asleep. I opened my eyes and looked up at her. She said, "You two had better be getting married after you get back from finding your...," she stopped in midsentence and realized we weren't in bed together. She said, "I thought you two were a couple. Why are you sitting in a chair beside her?"

"Mom, I care for her a lot, but I'm not ready to commit to any woman right now," I said as I stroked Kat's hair.

"Jason, she looks at you like you hung the moon and stars. Is she a good person?"

"Yes, Mom, she is wonderful. She's smart, good-natured, and a hard worker. She's also stubborn, opinionated, and drives me crazy at times."

Mom looked at me and said, "Sounds like love to me."

"Mom, that's not helping me move away from her."

"Son, it's obvious to everyone else that you love her. Why fight it?"

Being outmatched and outgunned, I changed the subject. "Do you think I can find Michael? That's a lot of territory between here and St. Louis."

"Your Dad will be going with you. If anyone can find him, you two can. Please don't take Kat with you when you leave. I'd like to get to know her."

Thank God, Kat woke up and heard Mom because I didn't want Kat to go along with me. Kat hugged Mom. "Mrs. Walker, I'd like to stay with you and get to know Jason's family and friends, but Jason needs me to protect him."

"You're sharing a room with my son, so I guess you need to call me Mom. Jason says you're good at surviving and you saved his butt several times. I'd like you to be my personal guard while Jason and his father are gone. Please?"

Kat looked at me. "Jason?"

I replied, "As much as I like your company, you need the rest, and Mom needs the protection."

"I guess your dad can watch your back while I stay with Mom."

My only thought was, *"Oh shit! This is starting to backfire on me. I'll be married and have six kids if Mom and Kat get together and plot against me!"*

***

Tina's smell was strong and made MMax want to find her. He whined to get his human's attention, but Jason couldn't hear him over the din of the other humans. MMax heard Tina bark and was very happy to see her again. He looked up at Jason and begged to join her. He was soon rewarded with the command to go. He ran to her, and they ran and romped for a short time. They were quickly exhausted and lay together in the barn. MMax licked Tina's muzzle and loved being close to her. He'd been with Jason and on missions since he was only a few months old and had never had the company of other dogs. He was happy.

☆

Chapter 16

The Walker place, Walter Hill, Tennessee.

MMax and Tina lay in the barn for several hours resting and then slept for a short time until the wind shifted. The odor hit MMax's nose like a sledgehammer. He could never forget that vile odor from the evil one. He stood up and left the barn. MMax looked around the area to the north and found the smell came from a stand of trees on a hillside. He started to go find the evil one, but Tina blocked him and licked his face.

MMax led Tina to the house and barked until the nice lady let Tina and him into the home. He whined outside his human's door, but the nice lady told him to be quiet. He wanted Jason to go with him to kill the evil one. It wouldn't happen that night.

***

Mom served a great breakfast, and all of us pitched small table scraps to MMax and Tina. Mom said, "Your dog is very smart and well behaved. He wanted in your room last night, but I told him to give Kat and you some alone time, and he went to sleep in our room."

I felt terrible because, for the second time in years, I hadn't thought about my best friend. I had been preoccupied with Kat. MMax had spent the evening with Tina, so I knew he wasn't lonely. I just hoped he was better with women than I had been over the years.

Kat was busy stuffing her face but said, "MMax is the best dog ever. He is becoming my best friend. Well, besides Jason."

Mom stared as Kat shoveled another biscuit and jelly into her mouth. I noticed she was in awe of how much the girl could eat. "Mom, Kat lost a lot of weight when she was captured a few months back and says she's trying to regain her lost weight. I think she just likes good home cooking. I've never seen her eat like this before."

MMax placed his head in her lap and begged for another piece of bacon.

Everyone asked Jason and Kat about their adventures, and they told them everything except how gruesome the children were killed. Most appreciated the hard decisions Jason and Kat had made on fighting back and killing people. However, Sister Joan was aghast at the killings. She couldn't wrap her head around the need to kill to survive. Kat started to mention a tough guy who Jason had dealt with, she said, "and Jason …"

Sister Joan slapped her hands to her head. "Stop! Killing is sinful and murder! I have to get away from this!" she said as she stormed out the door and across the field to the woods.

Kat started to follow her, but Father James stopped her. "Give her time. She has to deal with her beliefs for a while before I give her counseling."

Later that night, we sent a search party out to find Sister Joan without success. The prevailing thought was that she had simply walked away to find peace from all the killing. Dad and I knew she would probably be dead or captured by FEMA in a few days. No one wanted to sacrifice their lives to mount a major search.

Dad was thrilled to see the old tools I'd found on the way home. He was beside himself when Kat gave him the handful of books on woodworking using the antique tools. "Thanks so much for the tools. We'll need them to rebuild our way of life. I have something to show you."

Mom said, "Let's let the men play with their tools while I take you around and introduce you to everyone."

They left with Mom towing a reluctant Kat away from the barn. Dad took me to his workshop and proudly showed me what he had accomplished since the lights went out. I was surprised to see a shaft running across the ceiling, anchored in bearings every two feet. There were several pulleys spaced out along the metal shaft. Dad pointed to an ancient hit and miss engine on the far end of the shop on the floor. It had a belt going from a round, shiny thing on the engine to the shaft above.

I walked over to the engine. "Dad, what's that thing with the pulley attached to it?"

"Son that thing is a centrifugal clutch from a golf cart. You can't just start the engine and let her rip. That would burn my drive belts as the pulleys slipped."

"That was a stroke of genius."

Dad chuckled and said, "I saw this arrangement on one of those PBS shows on how old-timers made furniture. They had a steam engine and a set of clutches similar to what a car has. I don't have metalworking tools, so I improvised. That reminds me, we need to scavenge for more clutches and other items to make more of these Rube Goldberg machines. I want to expand by generating electricity and metalworking."

Dad showed me how one belt turned a drill fast enough to drill steel or wood. He had grinders, lathes, and saws powered by this maze of pulleys. OSHA would have shut him down in a skinny minute. That is, if they still existed.

I thought for a few minutes. "Dad, don't we need to get some old trucks and cars working? I remember a cartoon about Hillbillies up in Kentucky who had a truck up on blocks that had a belt running from a wheel rim to a sawmill. A truck engine would have a lot more power than an old putt-putt engine."

Dad slapped me on the back. "That's why I keep you around! Well, besides killing bad guys and other hero stuff."

"Thanks for the compliment. Hey, when are we leaving to find Michael and his family?"

"I'm surprised you want to leave that beautiful young lady here alone after what happened with Karen."

That was a sore topic, and I started to smart off to my dad but thought better of it. "Dad, Karen and I never meant much to each other. Oh, I liked her and wanted to pursue a relationship but oh well…"

"Son, what about Kat? You seem to have mixed emotions about her."

I shook my head and played with the stubble on my chin. "I think you described my dilemma. Kat loves me, and I'm warming up to her. Maria was only friends with benefits, and I had stopped seeing her before TSHTF. I started caring for Karen and her kids, so I tried not to get attached to Kat. Karen is a mature woman where Kat is still kinda immature and impetuous. Do you get what I'm saying?"

"I do. You want Kat for fun and Karen to settle down with because you want a partner in life that is closer to your own mental maturity. Well, grow up. Karen is with Murph, and you have a young woman who adores you. I'll bet Kat would have never given up on you and moved on to another man. That's all I have to say about that."

"Thanks for the advice. Now, when are we leaving?"

Dad spent the next two days, making sure everyone knew what to do in his absence. He took Maria off to the side and asked her to focus on their survival and place her love life on hold during her stints at guard duty. His talk with Pete wasn't so polite, and Pete left promising to never be caught with his pants down again.

205

Both Karen and Maria tried to catch me alone, but I made sure I either avoided them or had Kat clinging to me. I never said it aloud, but I felt betrayed by Karen and jealous of Murph. Murph did ask man-to-man to discuss the situation. We talked, and I let him off the hook. I told him I was now with Kat and that Karen had thought I died. I added that Karen was a great lady, and he should be proud that she would have anything to do with the likes of him. It made him feel better; me, not so much.

The two days passed quickly, and I avoided sleeping in the bed with Kat. The chair wasn't comfortable, but I'd slept well in worse conditions. Kat walked back from the bathroom with a robe on. She closed the door behind her and dropped her robe to the ground. My eyes bugged out as she lay down on the bed and looked so inviting.

I dressed quickly when she asked me to join her. Tears came to her eyes, and then she started blubbering. "You only want Karen, don't you?"

I placed my hand on her shoulder and said, "No, I want you."

"Then get in bed with me, now."

"No, I can't. Kat, I'm not a good person, and you need to move on and find a man worthy of you."

Through the tears, I heard, "I don't care what's bugging you. I want you to love me and be with me."

"I can't," I said and left the room. I walked down the hall and passed my mom on the way to the barn. Mom stopped me. She said, "You know your dad, and I heard every word of that conversation."

"Oh, crap!"

"Son, what do you mean by you're not a good person?"

I hadn't discussed the worst day of my life with anyone but Maria since it had happened two years ago. "Mom, maybe one day I'll be able to talk about it. All I have to say is I did something stupid and got three of my buddies killed and four others wounded. No one but Maria and I know how much we fouled up. Please don't ask. I'll sleep in the barn. Mom, help her move on and introduce her to a good guy who will take care of her."

"Jason. Jason! Get your butt back here," Mom said as I walked out the back door to the barn.

The next morning, Dad and I saddled our horses and prepared to leave. Kat didn't come out of her room. Mom hadn't spoken to me all morning, other than to say good morning and pass the gravy. Now, I had two of the women I cared for ready to skin me alive. I tried not to piss my sister off that morning, so at least there would be one woman happy to see me when … well, if I returned.

Dad and I said goodbye to everyone and were ready to mount our horses when Kat burst from the house, ran to me, and launched herself into the air. She knocked me back into my horse as she wrapped her arms and legs around me. She almost started a small stampede when my horse was startled. She kissed me about ten times in five seconds and whispered in my ears. "Jason, I love you, and I don't care what happened in your past. I'll be waiting for you when you get back. I'm not Karen."

She kissed me again, and I got carried away and kissed her passionately. Yeah, crap. In ten seconds, everything I did to run her off was ruined by one careless moment of lust. I'm sure glad Dad and I were leaving, or I would have carried her to the bedroom.

MMax was by Kat's side as I stuck my foot in the stirrup. "Come on, MMax. Let's go."

He looked up at Kat, and she dropped to her knees and hugged him. I had to say, "Heel," before he joined me beside my horse. I think my dog had fallen for Kat. I looked back and smiled at Kat and Mom. Mom punched Kat in the arm, and they both hugged. I wondered what the heck that was about but had other things on my mind that day.

I need to retrain MMax and show him who his boss was. He trotted beside us as we rode away. I felt sorry for him every now and then and placed him across my lap to rest. I think he preferred to walk but laid in my lap just to please me. MMax, Dad, and I had started on a much larger adventure than we ever would have guessed. I'll never forget leaving or the welcome I received when we came back.

Of course, Dad started pumping me for the reason why I didn't think I was a good person. I told him that I would tell him the whole story, but only if he didn't tell anyone, even Mom. Darn those thin walls at Dad's home.

Okay, that's all the mushy stuff for now. It's time to get back to finding my brother, traveling to new places, and killing bad guys. Something I'm good at doing. I look back at what I've written about my early days, and even I realize that I'd be piss poor at writing a romance novel. The mushy stuff happened, and I think I'd be remiss in not sharing the stuff that's fit to print. Of course, I left off the juiciest parts because my friends and wife might actually read this manuscript one day. Now, back to finding my brother and his family.

On Highway 24 heading to Nashville, TN

"Dad, we have as much a chance of finding Michael as a blind man in a paintball fight. Is this just a way to get Mom off your back?"

"Our chances are better than you think. Michael called me about three o'clock in the afternoon before the crap hit the fan. He said they were leaving then and should arrive before midnight. I think he made it at least to just north of Nashville. He would be on Highway 24, so we need to go the way he would travel and count on a bit of luck to find him."

My mouth opened before my brain engaged. "Well, that makes me feel better. We only have around a hundred miles of I 24, and a million miles of backroads, dirt roads, and cow paths to search."

The silence was unnerving. Dad stopped his horse and stared at me. "Did that worthless but obvious statement make you feel better?"

The words I uttered were very feeble. "No, sir."

"Do you think they made me feel better?"

"No, sir."

Dad smiled, "Now that you got that constipated thought out of your anal canal, can we continue our search for your brother, or do you want us to sit under a shade tree waiting for your mom to think that we've been out long enough and go home without Michael?"

Dad took a deep breath and waited for me to say something stupid. "Dad, you know I will search for my brother until the world ends ..."

Dad gave the time out sign. "Son, poor choice of words. Go on."

"I won't stop until we find him, or die trying. I just was stating the odds of ever seeing him again."

"Thanks for clarifying. Son, I don't want to trade one son's life for another, but we can't quit before we start. Now let's move on and keep an eye out for obvious signs that Michael might have left for us to find."

Again, that 10-watt lightbulb flickered in my brain. "Dad, do you think Michael remembered what you said about when you're lost in the woods to leave signs in the trees to point the direction you are traveling?"

"You remembered, and Michael will also."

I started to open my mouth and say, *"What if a thousand other fathers taught their kids the same thing?"*

As though he read my mind, Dad said, "Most people won't use beer cans to point the way."

I thought, *"Damn, he's good at this father stuff. I hope to be as good as him with my kids."*

We planned to travel all the way to Grand Rivers on Highway 24 looking for Michael or signs that he had left. The going was slow due to the need to keep a low profile and hide from people. We couldn't ride at night if we wanted to watch for signs that my brother had left, but moving during daylight was much more dangerous. Most people we encountered were harmless and just trying to get by day-to-day. Several groups begged for food, but Dad turned them away. One small group wanted one of our horses to eat.

Dad said, "Sorry, these horses are our only means of transportation. Don't you have gardens?"

"No, that's too much work. We'll take both your horses if you don't give us one."

MMax growled, and I said, "Watch him." Dad surprised me by drawing his .45 ACP and shooting the two closest men. I reacted and dropped the other three with 9mm bullets. They only got off one shot before they died. MMax sprang into action when he saw another man wield a machete and swing it toward my head. MMax jumped and bit the arm holding the machete before dragging the man to the ground. I yelled, "Bite him!"

MMax obliged and chomped down harder on the man's arm. The guy cried as he begged me to call off my dog. I threw the machete into the woods and kneeled beside the thug. "So, you planned to eat my horse? Ya know, MMax hasn't been fed in a couple of days. MMax, old buddy, how does this man taste? Do you want him for supper?"

The man lunged to his feet to flee but only succeeded to rip his arm wide open since MMax still had his teeth sunk into the man. I saw the blood gush from the man, and his face turned white. He said, "Please save me. Apply a tourniquet. Please."

I laughed at the man and said, "MMax, out."

MMax released his grip, and I said, "Watch him."

MMax stood ready to bite as the man closed his eyes for the last time.

Dad said, "Son, check their weapons and take any worth having. Search the bodies for anything useful."

"Yes, sir."

I didn't find anything worth having and pitched the guns in the woods after pocketing the bullets. "Dad, we need to find some good people to ask about Michael along the way."

Dad replied, "Yep, we do, but that exposes us to crap like them. Let's roll."

I saw a red stain on Dad's shirtsleeve. "Dad, you were hit by a lucky shot from those men I killed. Let me look at it."

"I did, It's just a scratch and has stopped bleeding."

"Damn it, Dad, even a small scratch can get infected," I said as I tossed him a tube of Neosporin. Then I added, "Dad, we're going to travel through the suburbs of Nashville and will be sitting ducks on these horses. We need some body armor. Let's stop at some police stations along the way and try to find some vests."

Dad was silent for a minute. "It's too damned hot for body armor."

I started to say that it was too damned deadly not to wear body armor. "Dad, I wore body armor during my tours in Afghanistan, and it was 984 degrees in the shade. It saved my life several times."

"Hummmph, 984 degrees. Okay, we'll drink a lot of water."

***

The Walker place, Walter Hill, Tennessee.

Ray saw the two men and the vicious dog leave. This pleased him and fit well into his plans. He'd been watching the house for several hours each day, waiting on his chance to attack. He smiled when he thought about how lucky he was to have captured the nun. She was beautiful without the habit on. He'd made her dress in shorts and a halter-top. She was chained to a post in his small living area. She would bring him many days of joy until he captured the other women.

Ray knew he had to do something quickly because they kept adding people to the group. He was thankful most were women and children that could be sold or kept for his own amusement.

Ray wasn't very smart but did know how animals reacted in the woods when he tracked and killed them. Just as though a mother rabbit leads the predator away to protect the little bunnies, Ray would lead many of them on a wild goose chase and then circle back for the kill. He had thought about nothing else for the past few weeks.

★

Chapter 17

South of Nashville, Tennessee on Highway 24.

We rode on as though we'd just performed a routine daily task like taking out the garbage. The killing was getting easier by the day, and I hated it. I thought killing would be behind me once I'd left the warzone. Now, the entire world was a warzone. We definitely needed the armor. We made a side trip over to the center of Smyrna to check out the police station but were shocked by what we saw. The entire center of the city had been burned to the ground. We didn't understand how there could be such utter devastation until I saw the engine and tail assembly of a super jumbo Boing 977 at the southeast side of the town hall. The Fed X jet must have had a full load of fuel when it crashed into the city.

The worst part of what we saw was that people were picking through the burned outbuildings to find valuables and food. Every time someone found something, the crowd gathered around them and fights broke out. We quickly rode away from the area in hopes no one would see us. We were too late. A woman yelled, and every head turned our way. I stopped and reached down to pick MMax up. The streets were littered with glass and jagged metal. He couldn't avoid being cut if he needed to run full speed.

We rode away at a good trot to avoid hurting the horses, but the crowd was still behind us, and we heard gunshots. A bullet shattered a window in front of us and pissed me off. I stopped and leveled my rifle at them. I took aim and fired three times. The leading three men fell to the ground. All three were gut shot. The vermin kept coming so I shot five more times killing four more of the filthy men and women. The rest tucked tail and disappeared into the shadows. Dad and I headed north on Highway 41 to LaVergne.

LaVergne was a different story. We were met by armed citizens and a Deputy Sheriff. The Deputy Sheriff asked, "Who are you, and why are you trying to enter our city?"

Dad replied, "I'm Zack Walker from Walter Hill, and that's my son Jason. We're searching for my other son and his family. They were heading to Walter Hill from St Louis."

The man had a sour look on his face. "Then you need to be on Highway 24 and get out of our town."

Before Dad could speak, an old truck drove up. It had the word 'Sheriff' painted on the doors. A large man got out and said, "Zack, is my deputy giving you a hard time?"

Dad walked up to the Sheriff. "No, Ezra, he's just doing his job. My son and I are searching for Michael and his family."

Ezra said, "Why I haven't seen your kids since eighth-grade football."

I looked at the huge black man who had played linebacker for the Nashville Packers and said, "I'm Jason. I played running back for you."

"I recognized you when I drove up. You're bigger but look the same. Last I heard, you were killing Arab terrorists over in the sandbox."

"I killed them all and was sent to Europe to kill more terrorists. We couldn't kill them fast enough to save Europe," I replied.

Most Arabs and Muslims were peaceful people. The damned Russian, Syrian, and Iranian governments taught the hatred for the west and supplied the millions of jihadists to the ever-expanding fight for civilization.

Ezra asked, "What can we do for you?"

My Dad said, "We need to borrow some body armor. We're riding the full length of Highway 24 from Nashville to 57, and every thug and starving person is taking potshots at us."

Ezra snickered, "Hell, man. I got some extra vests and a couple of old ARs you can have. I can give you about a hundred bullets. I know it's not much, but it's all I can spare."

"Thanks, Ezra. You are a good man," I said.

Ezra shook our hands. "I have to say, your largest problem will be the people who will shoot your horses just to get some fresh meat. People are starving out there."

"I guess we'll have to take our chances."

Ezra said, "No man left behind. Hooah!"

Dad and I both answered, "Hooah!"

Ezra gave us the arms and equipment, and his wife gave us two bags with a ham, two loaves of homemade bread, and some canned goods. Ezra said, "Can I talk you into spending the night here? I have some JB Black with your name on it."

Dad replied, "I'd like some whiskey, but I can't help but think that Michael and his family are in danger and need our help. Thanks for your hospitality, but we really need to go."

Northwest of Nashville, Tennessee on Highway 24.

I guess the part of our trip that I'll always dread was the trip through Nashville on Highway 24. We knew from the start, this would be the most dangerous, and even Dad questioned the chance of both of us being killed to save my brother. It's hard to describe Nashville a few months after the grid went down. Watching a Mad Max movie would help get one ready for the destruction of the city and the deprivation.

The bulletproof vests were hot as Hell and not as good as I had in the Army, but they would stop most handgun and low caliber rifle bullets. I was still used to wearing the equipment and sweating so much you had to drink water constantly or die of dehydration. Dad, on the other hand, bitched about the vests. I know it was mean, but I acted like it was no big deal and told Dad he needed to chill out.

Dad heard me say chill out and said, "I'll stick your chill out up your ..."

We were just northwest of Highway 24 and Highway 65 split when Dad was interrupted by gunfire coming from the western side of Highway 24. We got off the highway and rode down the embankment to a row of stores. Before we could react, several bullets hit a building fifty feet away. Then, bullets hit in front of us. They weren't aimed at us but had us trapped. I rode to a store and pushed the door open. I jumped off my horse and led him into the building. MMax and Dad followed me into the building, which turned out to be a mattress shop. We took the horses to the back of the store and waited for the gunfire to cease before sneaking out the back door.

The scene in the alley behind the store was sickening. There were a dozen bodies with their arms cut off. A few were still alive but bleeding out. We couldn't do anything to help the poor wretches, so we got the heck out of there as fast as we could. We found ourselves riding north on Westcap Road with homes dotted on either side. We hit the end of the paved road and continued on a dirt road for several miles until we came to a big house that faced Lickton Pike.

"Son, that home has a pool with a cover on it. The owners didn't get a chance to uncover it for the summer. Let's see if any water is left. I don't trust streams that flow through built-up areas. Our LifeStraws can't filter out everything. Heavy metals, viruses, and some parasites can get through."

I laughed. "Dad, you're preaching to the choir. Our military versions were much better, but we rarely used them. You had a better chance of dying from a case of water dropping on your head than dying of thirst. The Army did a great job of keeping us supplied. We owned the air, but the ground was always shifting sand."

I took the lead in sweeping the area for people or other dangers. The area was close to the highway but deep in a dense section of woods. I walked around the perimeter while Dad fed the horses. The house was actually on a twenty to thirty-acre estate. There were a large horse barn and a two-acre lake north of the home. The barn was hidden from the home by a double stand of pine trees. The lake looked clean and actually had a hundred foot long white sandy beach complete with a pavilion, dock, and diving board. I could live here. Then I thought, *It's abandoned. I should talk Dad into moving us up here.*"

As has become too frequent, my thoughts of a good life were interrupted by a scream from the woods. "MMax, search."

I had MMax on a leash and followed closely behind him. We cut across a well-worn path, and MMax doubled back and took it east. We'd only traveled a hundred yards through the brush and woods before MMax stopped and pointed at several people. Two men and a woman were tying a girl's hands behind her. Another woman lay on the ground. The men had black uniforms and M4 rifles. The rifles were leaning against a tree while they struggled with the belligerent girl.

I told MMax to be quiet and led him closer to the people. The woman kicked one man in the groin, and he fell to the ground. I didn't expect this, but drew my knife and jumped from the bushes. I grabbed the other man by his face and twisted it sideways as I pulled my knife across his throat. Then I said, "Get her," to have MMax attack the lady with a gun in her hand. I thought, "*Damn, I didn't see the gun,*" as I turned to the man on the ground. He was turned away from me and had both hands holding his groin.

I heard screaming behind me as MMax worked his magic but ignored the noise. The woman must have landed a mighty kick to the man's privates because he died without ever taking his hands from his groin. I wiped my knife on his shirt and then turned to see the woman trying to beat MMax on the head with her free hand, and MMax using his strength and training to keep her at bay. Hell, most people don't struggle when a Belgium Malinois clamps his teeth down on their arms.

Her gun lay by her feet, so she dropped down to the ground ignoring the excruciating pain. MMax was a bit smarter than the woman was and only had to drag her a few feet away from the gun, which I retrieved. The two captured women lay on the ground with their hands tied behind them. One said, "Are you going to set us free or take us for your own?"

This kinda caught me in a funny way, and I laughed aloud. The woman said, "That's not funny, mister. Let us go or shoot us, we're not going to be anyone's play toy."

I laughed and said, "Look, ladies. If you resist kicking me in the nuts, I'll set you free. The last time I rescued a woman about to be molested, I got stuck with her and can't get rid of her. So suffice it to say, you are free to go when I release you."

I cut their bindings and helped them to their feet. "What happened? I think these are FEMA thugs. What did you do to piss them off? What was this woman's role in abducting you?"

The feisty one said, "We didn't do anything but tell them to screw themselves when they said we had to relocate to one of their camps. The damned woman tricked us into thinking they were going to help our friend who had been wounded. She finds people for them and is rewarded. They killed the three men we were traveling with, and we quickly figured out what they planned to do to us. That's when you showed up."

I walked over to the woman who was still fighting with MMax. "What drugs are you on? No one can take that much pain."

"Go to hell!" were her last words. I cut her throat and said, "MMax, out!"

MMax released her arm, and she died with her comrades. The two ladies cringed at my actions. "Did you have to kill her?"

Before I could speak, Dad came up cautiously through the bushes. "Son, is everything okay?"

"Yes, Dad, I just helped these two ladies with an issue. They're okay now."

Dad saw the men and woman and said, "Looks like FEMA trash. What did the woman do to piss you off? Crap, MMax almost tore her arm off."

"Dad, the woman tricked these two women and their friends into meeting with the FEMA crud. The bastards killed their friends and then planned to … well … you know the rest."

The woman who hadn't spoken said, "We need to thank your son for freeing us. You can't blame us for being afraid of you. Most men we've run into have only one thing on their minds."

Dad looked at the two and said, "Darn, Jason, you never rescue ugly women. Do you have some kind of radar to find these beauties in need of help?"

I shifted my feet and fiddled with my hands as I said, "I just have a knack for this kinda stuff."

Dad said, "Sorry for your loss. What do you plan to do now without your husbands or boyfriends?"

The loudmouthed girl said, "We barely knew them. We were on a trip to the Bahamas when the crap hit the fan and were stuck at the Nashville Airport. There were twenty-eight of us when we started heading north months ago. Most of our companions were killed or captured. We were lucky and found a nearby farmer who let us work on his farm for food and a place to sleep."

Dad asked, "Are you afraid of hard work? Are you willing to work to help feed yourselves and our little community? We have about thirty people living on a farm south of Nashville out in the sticks. We don't plan to abuse you or make you slaves, but you will find it safe and will get plenty of food if you contribute to the community."

I wanted to tell Dad that we had women coming out our ears and needed some men to help with the heavy work and fighting. I kept my mouth shut because it was his farm, and he was a good man trying to help.

The women went off by themselves to talk while Dad and I searched the FEMA thugs for anything useful. We found two Sig 9mm pistols, several knives, the two M4s, and their tactical vests. Dad also stripped them of their clothes and shoes. As we worked, I said, "Don't we need to find some men to balance the community out a bit?"

Dad chuckled, "You don't like to be surrounded by pretty women?"

"Dad, I like women as much as the next guy and have fought and bled with some of the best female fighters in the world, but sometimes you need brute strength."

Dad quickly replied, "Several weeks ago, I began to notice that men are disappearing from the earth at an alarming rate. We might not have a choice on who joins us. Men are out scrounging for food to keep their families alive. They're fighting gangs, criminals, and neighbors every day for every scrap of food. I'll bet there are three women for every man left alive on this planet, and it will get worse."

I knew he was right and what he'd said made me think. "Dad, the women who are left might be alive, but just barely. Many still have kids to feed, and bad men abusing them without a husband or boyfriend to share the load. I hope they band together and fight for survival. This damned country is going to the dogs."

"Son, that's why we'll help anyone who needs help. Your mom and I want to train as many women how to survive as possible. Life is hard now. Most won't survive this coming winter. I want us to grow fast and get prepared to fight off much larger groups. Maria and some of the other women need to step up and get these women trained."

We heard MMax warn us that the ladies were coming back to join us, and we turned toward them. The meek one said, "You saved our lives and didn't rape us, so we don't have much choice but to join you."

Dad's jaw moved, but he was speechless. I said, "Ma'am, you always have choices. You can go out on your own. We'll give you some food and guns to protect you. If you come with us, life will still be hard, but I promise no one will touch you unless you want to be touched, and we'll train you to fight and protect yourself. Our head of training is a fellow soldier, Maria McGill. We soldiered together all over the Middle East and Europe. You won't find anyone tougher or better at training people to defend themselves and to fight. My mom and girlfriend, Kat, will teach you how to work on the farm. Sorry for rambling, but we need you as much as you need us. Only a well-armed, well-trained, force can survive this mess in the long run."

Both ladies felt much better about joining our group, but they were put off when Dad told them that we would go on and find my brother before returning to take them to the farm. We gave them most of our food, two pistols, and helped them settle in the large home before leaving the next day. We were sorry the ladies were upset but reminded them they were not tied up and being passed around to pleasure a bunch of thugs. The loud one told me she didn't think they would ever see us again.

I said, "If we're alive and if you're here, we'll pick you up in two to three weeks to take you home with us. I promise."

☆

Chapter 18

Northeast of Nashville on Highway 24.

The next week dragged on as we slowly traveled from Nashville heading northwest following Highway 24. We not only had to watch for danger from people but also had to look out for signs from Michael and his family. We ran into several gangs and thugs along the way and chose to hide from them whenever possible. This was difficult since we needed to travel in broad daylight. MMax stayed busy pointing out ambushes and people in our path. He saved our butts numerous times, and I wouldn't be alive now if not for him. I love that dog.

I'm ashamed to say that it was hard to focus on security, Michael's signs, and missing Kat. Yes, I missed her. She was the biggest pain in my ass in my entire life, but I missed her. I missed the smell of her hair as it touched my cheek when we rode double. Yep, I hesitate to say it, but I missed her skinny body against mine on horseback and in bed. Maybe we were meant for each other. Well, that was Good Jason speaking. Bad Jason thought about her every night, but we won't discuss those thoughts.

Crap, I was thinking about Kat when I accidentally glanced to my right, and a glint of something shiny caught my eye. The beer cans were stuck in a cottonwood tree about ten feet up, which was just high enough for them to be too much trouble to remove. I pointed to them. "Dad, look! Those could be Michael's handiwork!"

Dad rode up to them and looked at the cans. He pulled one from the tree. "Jason, this one has a note rolled up around the tree limb."

He untied the note and then unrolled it. He read it aloud. "Dad or Jason, I knew you would come to find us. Head southeast on Highway 24 as far as it is from our farm to the Jenkin's place. Take a left and go as far as it is from our barn to the dirt road west of the barn. We'll be waiting. My foot is injured, and we had to hole up for a while. Everyone is alive and getting thinner."

Dad dismounted and said, "Jason, watch our backs while I make a map from Michaels instructions."

It was summer now, and hot as hell in Tennessee and Kentucky. The concrete shimmered from the heat, and the flies were biting, so I figured a storm was heading our way. The flies weren't as bad as those little black SOB mosquitoes. "Dad, can you hurry up? These little black bastards are eating my hands and neck up."

Dad ignored me and kept doodling on his notebook. I noticed he swatted at something on his neck twice and then his horse took out down the road. He didn't say anything and just left me swatting those little boogers. I kicked my horse and took off behind him, hoping the breeze would blow the mosquitoes away. I kinda sorta knew where Dad was heading and was surprised when he blew by the overpass where we should have left the highway. I caught up to him and said, "We're going past the turnoff to make sure no one is following us, right?"

"Yep," was all he said.

I scouted the area to my left as we rode by but didn't see anything noticeable. The woods were thick, and an army could be hiding in them without being seen. We rode down the entrance ramp on the east side of the highway and hid in a copse of trees. MMax was breathing heavy with his tongue hanging out. I dismounted and gave him some water. This heat was especially bad on the horses and MMax. Dad and I cursed the heat, flies, and mosquitoes but knew we had it made compared to the animals. Most of the time, MMax chose to walk rather than ride across the saddle, due to comfort issues. I needed to figure that one out before taking MMax on any long rides.

Time passed slowly as we watched for anyone trying to follow us. I also noted that only a few people passed us on the highway. They were mainly families heading to some other place where they thought they could find safety or more food. Well, that's what Dad and I thought. I saw one group that tugged at my heartstrings. A man and woman walked along with two kids about ten and eleven years old. The man pushed a wheelbarrow, and everyone had a backpack to carry their food and possessions.

One of the boys pulled away from his mom, ran up to his dad, and pulled on his hand. The boy said something and the man yelled loud enough that we could hear him a hundred feet away. The man yelled again and slapped the boy, who ran back to his mom. I raised my rifle and placed the man in the middle of my sights. Just before I was going to squeeze the trigger, my dad pushed the barrel up in the air. I gave him a dirty look.

"Son, unless you plan on taking in a woman and two more kids don't shoot the only man taking care of them and feeding them. The kids are clean, they're not too scrawny, and they could be much worse off without this man in their lives."

"I'm sorry, Dad. I just can't stand anyone who abuses kids or women."

Dad chuckled as they walked out of sight down the hillside. "Son, I tried my best to set a good example of what a father should and shouldn't do for you kids. Apparently, I had a bit of success with you. If the world weren't so screwed up, I would have taken the shot and taken them to a shelter for abused women and children. Son, we can't help everyone, and we certainly can't take in all of the stray dogs."

"I know you're right, but it sticks in my craw that people like that man breath the same air as his kids. They will become abusive toward women and children when they grow up."

No one else came by for another hour, so we mounted our trusty steeds and rode north until Dad thought we were close enough to walk to my brother's hiding spot. The woods were thick with saplings and brush but not so thick that we had to cut our way through. We walked a couple hundred yards when MMax froze, pointing northeast of our position. We froze and could hear sounds in the distance that were unintelligible. We snuck up closer with MMax leading the way and almost walked into a clearing. We dropped to the ground.

The clearing was the size of a couple of baseball fields and had a small log cabin, outhouse, and old barn on the west end. There was a large garden by the house and a fenced in area with several cows, several mules, and some goats. There was a chicken coop beside the fenced in area. Two kids were hoeing the garden, and an old man was sharpening an ax on an old timey foot powered grinding stone. I saw one thing that piqued my interest the most. There was a cast iron old water pump at the back of the house by the kitchen door. I could fill all our water jugs with sweet well water.

Dad took his binoculars from their case and surveyed the area. He got excited. "That's your brother's kids, Jerry., and Sally! I don't know who the old … Hey, Pat just walked out of the barn. Darn, I don't see Michael. Let's walk up carefully. Raise your gun in the air along, with your other hand."

"Dad, let me go in while you cover me in a safe position."

"That's a great idea, son. You stay back and cover me."

I took up a position behind a tree and made sure Dad wouldn't cross my field of fire. I placed my sights on the man and was as ready as I could be. MMax sat beside me, sniffing the air. I rubbed his ears as Dad walked into the clearing.

No one saw Dad at first, then Jerry dropped his hoe and ran to the old man who raised a double barrel shotgun. The old man yelled, "Hold on there, Mac! Stop, or I'll fill yer britches with buckshot!"

Dad was over a hundred feet away and called out, "I'm Zack Walker and the kids' grandfather. I'm looking for my son Michael."

I saw Pat running toward Dad but couldn't hear what she yelled. Dad lowered his rifle to the ground and caught her when she collided with him. Pat wasn't a small woman, so both of them fell over to the ground. Then, both kids ran over and piled in on top of my dad. The old man lowered his shotgun, so I walked out of the woods with MMax leading the way. The old man saw me and raised his shotgun again. I raised my rifle over my head and slowly walked to him.

"I'm Jason Walker. Pat is my sister-in-law. Where's my brother?"

The old man said, "I'm Cletus McHenry, and you need to discuss her husband with her."

I was a bit confused, or dense as Kat always said. "Is Michael here or not?"

The old man pointed at Pat. "See Pat."

MMax growled, and I turned in time to tell MMax to stay just before my niece, Sally, and nephew, Jerry, bowled me over. All I heard was them screaming, "Uncle Jason! Did you bring us back something from the war?"

When they calmed down, I replied, "Yes, I brought you MMax and me. My plane crashed, and I lost everything else I owned."

I heard Dad growl. Yes, growl. Then he said, "Those sons a bitches will pay for this."

I instantly assumed that my brother had been killed by some thug or the other. "Dad, where's Michael? Why isn't he here?"

Dad was teary eyed and choked up, so Pat came over. She hugged me and said, "Michael's gone."

"What? Who killed him? I'm going to make them pay."

Pat hugged me tightly. "Calm down, Jason. We don't know if Michael's dead or alive. He sacrificed himself to allow us to escape from those FEMA thugs. He led them on a chase through the woods about two miles from here, and we saw them catch him. They probably have him working as a slave in a camp up in Kentucky or south Alabama."

I was getting madder by the second. "Which way did they take him? Dad, we have to go get Michael."

With tears still running down his cheeks, Dad said, "Son, they took him a month ago. He could be anywhere by now. Let's take Pat and the kids home and regroup."

"But, Dad!"

"Son, calm down and think things through. I know you could tear through the country and kill every FEMA agent in sight, until they send an army to kill you and probably the rest of us. We need a surgical strike that frees your brother and limits our exposure. Let's go home and make a plan to find out where the FEMA camps are located and then get intelligence on them."

I knew my dad was right, but I was still mad and wanted to kill something. That's what Army sergeants do. Officers think things through, plan, and, scheme before reacting. My dad was right about one thing. I had to calm down and think before I reacted in this screwed up world. In the Middle East and Europe, we'd always know who the enemy was and killed them all. If we accidentally killed an innocent person, God would handle sorting them out.

Leaving didn't go as smoothly as Dad and I had hoped. Pat wanted to stay at the old man's place, but the kids wanted to go home with us. Pat made the case that they were safe and had plenty of food. Even Cletus told her she was foolish to stay. He said, "Pat, there is plenty of food, but someday either FEMA or some starving bunch will find us. You will be safer with Zack and Jason. You and I can't fight anyone off."

Pat was in tears. "I know you're right. Will you come with us?"

"Girl, I was born in that cabin eighty-two years ago. My mom, dad, and three children are buried behind the barn along with my Sarah. We were married sixty-three years ago, and I ain't leaving her now. FEMA won't want me, and I can hide from anyone else until God calls me to join Sarah. You take the kids and go to Zack's home. Take plenty of food with you. You can take the wagon. Betsy and Jake will pull it to your new home. I'm getting too damned old to fool with those mules."

Pat asked, "Are you sure you won't come with us?"

He shook his head and said, "We'll load the wagon up this evening, and y'all can leave when Zack thinks it's safe."

Later, my dad pulled me away from loading the wagon. "Son, do you think we can make it home without a hundred people trying to take that wagon load of food away from us?"

I laughed, and Dad stopped me. "Jason, what's so funny."

"Dad, I read a post-apocalyptic book several years ago, and this older couple wanted to be able to drive their big lumbering truck full of supplies right through an area filled with starving people and gangbangers. They placed hazardous cargo signs all over the vehicle and wore hazardous chemical suits. No one stopped them. Let's see if Cletus has any red paint and white sheets."

Cletus had heard my plan and said, "I have changed my mind on the wagon and mules. Follow me to my garage."

He walked us around the barn to an old cinder block building and opened the sliding door. I was amazed. The building looked like a wreck on the outside but was neat and orderly on the inside. The walls had been painted white, and the floors were light gray, but that wasn't the big surprise. There was an old Ford sedan on one side of the garage and an old Dodge Power Wagon ambulance beside it.

I said, "That's an old Dodge Power Wagon."

Cletus said, "Kinda sorta. It's actually a 1958 Dodge M42 Ambulance. I purchased it from an Army-Navy store forty years ago. It runs on diesel and can go anywhere. I installed an extra fifty-gallon fuel tank, so we could drive it up to Alaska and back. We never made the trip, but I drove it for many years. I restored it ten years ago and only drive it in parades and sometimes on Sunday. Please, paint your hazmat signs on it and go safely home."

The ambulance had been painted back to its original OD green with the white circles with the red crosses in the middle. It would be easy for anyone not familiar with the current Army and FEMA vehicles to assume it was an official vehicle carrying hazardous material.

Dad said, "I hate to take a vehicle that means so much to you, but it could save all our lives. Do you have any fuel for it?"

"Yes, the tanks are full, and I have four five-gallon fuel cans to take with you. The old beast doesn't get outstanding fuel mileage, but you will have enough fuel to drive about seven-hundred miles without needing to find fuel. That extra fifty-gallon tank gives you about four hundred extra miles."

We spent the next day cutting a sheet of plywood into some squares for our hazardous signs. We painted the boards yellow and then added the word Caution at the top and the biohazard symbol in the middle of the remaining space. We placed one of those signs on the front and back of the vehicle. I had a brainstorm and made larger signs for the sides of the ambulance that had the word 'Caution' at the top, the biohazard symbol in the middle, and the words 'Human Remains' at the bottom.

I found a set of white vinyl stick on letters in Cletus's garage and stuck the words 'World Health Organization' on the top of the ambulance above the windshield. We stood back and looked at our work. Dad said, "Darn, if I wouldn't run the other way if I ran into this vehicle. Now we need to make it a bit more comfortable for our passengers and work on making some kind of official-looking uniforms."

Cletus slapped his side in joy. "I've got exactly what you need. I'll be back in a minute. Pat, bring the kids and follow me."

Dad and I removed all but two of the stretchers and most of the antique medical gear. We placed the items in a neat pile at the back of the garage. I looked around the inside and said, "This is just a tin box. It will be hotter than Hell if we don't insulate the walls and roof."

"I saw some three-quarter-inch foam insulation sheets in the barn. Cletus has about eight four-by-eight sheets of the stuff. Four would make a big difference," Dad said.

Cletus and the others came back loaded down with uniforms, old gas masks, and DC electric fans. He said, "These white medical uniforms will pass for hazmat suits, and the gasmasks will seal the deal. Wear these WWII tanker helmets and most people will swear you are hazardous material workers or space aliens. I'll wire the fans into the ambulance and cut some vent holes, so the passengers won't fry in the back."

Dad mentioned the insulation, and Cletus told us to take as much as we needed. We glued the insulation to the walls and back doors but had to bolt the sheets to the roof. The finished product looked rough until Cletus brought us some OD Green rattle cans to paint the insulation. He said, "Don't get it too wet, or the paint will melt the foam."

Six hours later, we were sure we had thought of everything to aid our trip when Cletus came out of his office with some paperwork. "These documents are your orders. All military and FEMA people have orders. I typed them up on my antique Underwood typewriter and made them look as authentic as I could. You know the military and other organizations don't have computers so they will have to resort to old technology. This should fool anyone but the highest level authorities."

I said, "Thanks so much for taking care of our family and helping us get back home safely. You need to come with us. You would be a great help to us with all your experience and ability."

Cletus smiled. "Thanks but no thanks. I'm going to stay with Sarah and get buried on my property."

Cletus would be dead before he ever saw the ambulance again. I went back to check on him the following year and found a friendly family had squatted on his property. They didn't know what had happened to the owner. I walked to the graveyard and smiled. Next to Sarah's grave was a new one with a marker that read, "Cletus Mc Henry, a good man."

***

Ray probed their defenses and found a couple of ways to penetrate the fences to get closer to the house. He knew he could get to the woman he wanted. If he were lucky, he'd get two or three others. He still had to figure out how to escape with three women in tow. He'd watched them for several weeks after Jason had left and saw something so obvious he slapped himself on the forehead. The women drove the old farm truck around the place at will but never left the area. He could kidnap the women, load them in the truck, and then drive away. They couldn't catch him on horseback.

Ray grinned through his rotten teeth and slapped his leg. He was excited and couldn't wait to capture Billie, the other woman, and her daughters. It was then, he took notice of the skinny blonde-haired young girl. She looked about fifteen, and he drooled when he thought about her coming to his place. He thought, "She will love me once she gets to know me. If she don't, I'll break her fool neck."

☆

Chapter 19

The Walker place, Walter Hill, Tennessee.

On the day Jason and his dad left, Kat spent the morning in Jason's old room. His mom had left it untouched since Jason had left for the Army. He was the youngest and only kid to have lived in the cabin. It was where Jason had spent his time when he was in town between deployments. Kat smelled his clothes and put on one of his t-shirts that had an Army logo on its chest. She checked all of his drawers but didn't find anything that would help her get to know Jason better.

Jan gave Kat a couple of days to recover and then showed her a list of her new jobs and responsibilities. Kat was eager to help her new community and shouldered the burden with a smile. She did encounter a few awkward moments with Billie and Karen but handled them very well. Karen asked her how she's met Jason, and Kat told her the truth; however, she's let Karen think they were madly in love. Kat never lied; she just let people assume and didn't correct their assumptions.

After supper on the fifth night, Jan began to ask intimate questions about Kat and her son's relationship. Kat blushed. "Mom, are you asking if I could be pregnant?"

Jan blushed, "I guess I was prying a bit too much. I'm sorry."

Kat reflected before answering. "Mom, that was a bit personal, but we're family now, and I know you want the best for Jason and any children he might have. The answer is yes it would be possible but look at this under my arm."

Kat showed her the bump from the birth control implant that Kat's mom had implanted in her by the family doctor. Her mom had thought Kat was promiscuous when Kat was actually backward about sex.

Jan felt the bump. "I think it's a good thing to avoid having kids now while the world is in turmoil, but don't wait too long. I want some more grandkids."

Kat said, "Jason doesn't want them now, but I plan to have a houseful later. I don't want kids to have to live through this mess now. We'll think about it again in about two years when this implant wears out."

Kat prayed every night that Jason would return and love her as she loved him. She was sure he had to miss her as much as she missed him. Kat also missed his goofy dog. She played with Tina some and took her on walks around the farm but still missed MMax and his goofy antics.

Jan, Michelle, and Kat soon became best friends, and Jan treated Kat like her second daughter. They met every evening after supper and played cards or just talked about the time before the bombs fell. Kat began to feel like part of the family. They were all about the same size and shared clothes and shoes. It was a good time for them, and they almost forgot the world had ended a few months back.

It was touch and go with Karen and Billie for the first week, and then they warmed up to Kat and her impetuous ways. Karen and Kat actually became good friends, and Missy and Chrissy went on long walks with Kat and Tina around the farm. Other than no electricity, TVs, cell phones, and video games, life was getting back to normal for the folks at the farm.

During one of their walks, they saw some people walking south on the road. Tina was back at the house, resting after playing with Kat earlier. They sought cover and watched as the group of half a dozen adults stopped to rest. Karen was close enough to hear them talking. She heard, "We can't rest long. The General's people will be in this area any day now, and I don't want to work on one of his farms."

One of the women said, "And I don't want to work in a brothel. We need some food. Let's raid the next farmhouse we come to today. These farmers always have food."

A man's voice said, "Bill, don't kill them this time. We might want to come back this way someday, and they'll have more food to take."

The people finished their break and continued walking south. Karen told the others, and the women checked their weapons and followed at a distance to make sure these people didn't find their farm. They were soon a half mile past the farm, and Kat said, "We need to attack them and wipe them out before they raid any of our neighbors."

Karen was astounded that anyone would think that way. Billie said, "Karen, you stay back here, so Kat and I can take care of them. Come on; let's get rid of the vermin."

Kat crossed the road and came up behind the people, so Billie and she could get them in a crossfire. Billie was to take out the man who appeared to be the leader, and Kat would take out the other man. That left the four women to deal with. Kat heard the shot and saw the leader grab his chest and fire. Kat shot the other man, just as the group turned to shoot in Billie's direction. Her man dropped to the ground with a bullet in his back. The bullet ripped his guts on its way through his body. The man was dead, but he didn't know it as he clutched his stomach.

The women panicked and shot in all directions as Kat and Billie shot from behind cover. They took careful aim and killed the four women. Kat walked up to the dead and dying and finished off the living. "That will teach you to raid innocent farmers. I hope God sends you straight to Hell."

Karen walked up as Kat fired the last shot into the gut shot man. She doubled over and vomited. "How can you shoot them in cold blood?"

Kat said, "Billie, come here. I want to say this one time, and then we'll never discuss it again. Karen, Billie, I was raped repeatedly by four FEMA assholes before I met Jason. I killed every one of them later. The day I met Jason, several men had killed my friend and tried to catch and rape me. I almost killed Jason thinking he was one of the men. Jason saved my life. I owe him and thank God every day for bringing him into my life.

Now, you don't need to be raped to know that killing these dregs of the earth that prey on innocent people is the right thing to do. I'll kill them every chance I get."

Both women stared at Kat with their mouths open. A minute later, they hugged Kat and cried with her. Karen sniffled and said, "I get it now. Give me time, and I'll help you rid the face of the earth of this vermin."

***

The three women didn't see Ray sneaking up on them, and Tina wasn't with them to sound an alarm. Just as he was about to pounce on them with guns drawn, the people could be heard. At first, he thought they were people from the farm and didn't want to tangle with that many of them. He felt safe getting the drop on three women. What he saw a few minutes later scared the crap out of him. Two of the women massacred the six people who were casually walking down the road. Ray saw the young, blonde girl walk among the wounded and shoot them in the head. Ray got the hell out of Dodge as fast as he could without making enough noise to alert the women.

Now, Ray knew not to take for granted that these women would be easy prey. He had to work on his kidnapping plan and ensure they didn't kill him.

***

Jan left the living room and came back with a bottle of homemade elderberry wine and two glasses. "Kat, I really like you, and I think you are perfect for my son. You wouldn't give up on him if he were away longer than expected."

"I love Jason with all my heart. If he was very late, I'd go find him."

"Find who?" Michelle asked as she walked into the room and then asked, "Where 's my glass?"

"It's in the cupboard. Sorry for not inviting you. Get a glass and join us. I'm getting to know my new daughter."

Michelle fetched a glass, and Jan filled it. Michelle probed Kat. "Jason told me about this woman he'd met a few days before finding me that drove him crazy. He said he'd only known her for two days, and she'd left him with aching balls but wanting to get to know her better."

Jan said, "Michelle, that's no way to talk."

Kat said, "Sorry, Mom, but Jason told her the truth. I fought him when he was trying to save me and kicked him in the shin and in the balls. I thought he was a rapist. He tackled me, knocked me to the ground, and then lay on top of me for a long time while MMax kept biting the stalker."

Tears came to her eyes as Kat remembered the FEMA men who had raped her before she met Jason. She said, "A couple of weeks earlier several, FEMA thugs caught me and ... well ... attacked me. I wasn't ready to be saved by a good man like my Jason. Anyway, I was mean to him and cursed at him to get off me. I was rude and nasty to him at first. I would have shot him if I'd had a chance. Then we talked, and I began to see what a decent man he appeared to be. I left him but followed him from a distance."

Kat went on to tell them about their exploits and mentioned several times about feeling safe in Jason's arms.

The wine made Kat sleepy, so she excused herself and went to her room. Jan and her daughter walked out on the deck to get some privacy. Jan said, "Kat and Jason's relationship is very confusing. It would make a great daytime soap opera."

Michelle looked up. "Huh, I think they make a great couple. She adores him and he, well, he's Jason. I can tell he loves her, but ... I don't know how to describe it."

Jan nodded. "Exactly, one minute they act like they're madly in love and the next, I heard Jason tell her to find another man because he isn't a good person."

"What? When did you hear Jason say that?"

"The day before he left, I thought they were making love and a bit noisy at that. It turned out to be Jason trying to break up with her. Jason left their bedroom and slept in the barn."

"Oh, shit."

"Watch it daughter."

"Sorry, well, they certainly kissed like lovers just before Jason left."

"Maybe Jason's heart will grow fonder. I really like this girl. Jason should too," Jan said.

"I love my brother, but since he became a dog handler, he just hasn't had much time for humans."

"He forgot about MMax several times while he was here."

"Mom, speaking of MMax, when will Tina deliver? I noticed she's sagging a bit, and I felt her puppies move this morning."

Jan pointed at Tina. "She should deliver in the next week or so. I hope the puppies don't look like mongrels. MMax is a good looking dog, and Tina is beautiful, but mixing their genes could deliver some pug ugly dogs."

★

Chapter 20

Northwest of Nashville, Tennessee on Highway 24.

We prepared to leave Cletus's home the next morning when Cletus handed a jar and two rolls of bandages to Pat. He said, "If anyone stops you along the way, pour this pig's blood on you and the children and wrap your arms or legs with the bandages. Act real sick. If they force you to open the doors, they will take one look and wave you to go on down the road. Nothing scares people like mentioning Ebola or Dengue Fever."

Pat kissed him on the cheek. "Cletus, you saved us, and I can never repay you but please keep our two horses. Perhaps you can trade them for something that you need."

"No need to worry about me. Just pay it forward. Help some other unfortunate family."

We pulled away with too much food, extra ammunition, and an ambulance all donated to us by Cletus. We'd tried to make the back end of the ambulance as comfortable as possible, but it was still hot and rough riding. We couldn't drive very fast, but at least with the windows rolled down and the vents open in the back, Pat and the kids could survive the ride to Dad's place.

We only encountered a few people on the drive to pick up the two women we had rescued from the FEMA thugs. Every one of the people who saw the ambulance stopped and read the signs before running or driving off the road to let us pass. The ruse worked much better than planned. No one shot at us, and no one challenged us. Dad got off Highway 24 and drove down the side roads until we arrived at the mansion in the woods.

We expected to be greeted as saviors and expected the two women to run up and hug us. Instead, several bullets hit the driveway in front of us and kicked gravel onto the ambulance. I started laughing at the situation. "Darn, this fake hazmat truck has fooled the women. Pat, give me a white cloth to wave."

I opened the door enough to poke out a stick with the white t-shirt and waved it before stepping out of the vehicle. "Hey, stop shooting. We came back to pick you up and take you home with us. The ambulance is a fake we decorated to keep people from attacking us."

The loud woman showed herself. "You almost got shot. We were scared to death you were bringing Ebola or something to us. Come on up."

Dad parked the truck, and everyone got out to meet the women. I said, "Sorry, we didn't get your names the other day. I'm Jason Walker; these people are my dad, Zack, my sister-in-law, Pat, and her two children."

The loud lady said, "I'm Heather Dill, and she is Darla Black. We honestly didn't expect you to come back to get us."

I said, "That's okay. These days it's hard to keep promises. We need you to gather your things and load them into the ambulance. I want to go through Nashville while the sun is up. This fake biohazard trick won't work in the dark. We'd have some jerk trying to steal our ambulance and shoot us full of holes before he could read the signs."

Darla said, "We can have all our stuff down here in fifteen minutes. We don't have much."

I asked, "Did the FEMA troops show up again?"

Heather said, "Yes, but we hid in the cellar. They only walked through the home and didn't find any people or food, so they left. We slept in the cellar and kept all of our stuff down there, so it was easy to fool them."

The women gathered their gear while the rest of us watched for strangers. We didn't see anyone, and the ladies returned and quickly loaded their gear into the ambulance. My niece and nephew lay on a pile of blankets on the floor, and the women sat on the uncomfortable wooden bench seat that ran the length of the driver's side in the back. I heard one of the women ask Pat if either Dad or I were married. I couldn't hear Pat's reply, but the lady said, "Too bad."

We drove back onto Highway 24 dodging stalled cars and other debris as usual when we saw a roadblock up ahead. We were only a mile or so from the Packer's stadium, and the barrier hadn't been there when we came through heading north. The men wore army fatigues and were armed with M4s. We had to take the bluff through to completion when they didn't crap their pants and wave us on through.

A man with sergeant stripes walked up to the ambulance but kept a healthy distance away. He asked, "What the hell are you doing, and where are you going?"

We had donned our gas masks when we'd first seen the barricade, so the man couldn't hear Dad's response. I opened my door and walked toward the man, lifting my mask as I walked. He said, "Stop, or I'll shoot!"

I said, "We're taking some bodies and a couple of live ones to the CDC in Atlanta. FEMA wants proof that the Syrians or Iranians launched a biological attack on several cities. They gathered the people in Indianapolis and asked us to come to fetch them. Boy, that was a mess. Millions of people died a horrible death when the virus consumed them. A hell of a way to die."

The sergeant backed up a couple of steps. "How do I know you're not a bunch of thugs trying to run guns or smuggle people past us."

I thumped the side of the truck and said, "I can open the backdoors and let you see the people. Well, what's left of them after Ebola and Hemorrhagic Dengue Fever gets through with them."

"Your story stinks to high heaven."

I remembered to show him the fake documents. "Here, read these."

I tried to hand the pages to him, but he made me hold them so he could read the small print."

"Open the doors!"

Of course, I was stalling to give the others time to apply their blood and bandages. I fiddled with the latch on the back door and opened one door. A bloody arm fell out, and the sergeant jumped backward several feet. "Open the other door."

The scene was gruesome. It would have fooled anyone but an expert on these diseases. The sergeant looked sick and struggled not to puke. "Close those doors and get your ass out of here. I'll report this to HQ tomorrow."

I said, "I've heard about him. Wasn't he a captain a short while ago?"

"Yes, he got a battlefield promotion according to our Lieutenant. He's one tough son of a bitch. Glad I don't have to work closely with him. Get on the road. Now!"

I lowered my mask and climbed back into the passenger seat. Dad took off as soon as they pushed the sawhorses away and sped down the road. I said, "Dad, I thought I had killed the man they call the General. He was a mean and nasty soldier in our unit who killed just to have fun. He was the one who teamed up with FEMA at that camp I escaped from after rescuing Michelle. He'll be looking for me to get even."

"Son, let's cross that bridge when we get to it. Let's get everyone home safe, and then we can figure out what to do about this so called General."

The sun was going down, and we cruised through Antioch looking for a wooded area to pull off the highway and spend the night. We couldn't afford being caught out after dark because no one could see our biohazard signs. We couldn't pull off at any intersections because this was a highly-populated area. We passed Haywood Lane, and I remembered there was a large stand of trees coming up ahead on the west side of the highway. I saw it a few minutes later and told Dad to slow down and pull off into the tree line.

He drove into the woods slowly, due to the rugged terrain and the thick undergrowth and bushes. "Darn it all. We're going to run out of the forest and into someone's backyard if we don't find a clearing pretty soon."

Little did Dad know that a few minutes later, that was precisely what happened. The low hanging branches and bushes scraped the windshield, making it impossible to see where we were going. Suddenly, we popped out of the brush and saw buildings blocking our path. The buildings meant people, and that scared me. I yelled, "Back up, Dad!" but I was too late.

We had the damnedest lousy luck to have driven right into a group of men in the middle of a pig roast with alcohol flowing. There was a copper still distilling moonshine, and most of them were smoking pot. All they saw was an Army green vehicle bust through the woods and charge at them. They must have thought it was a DEA bust. It must have scared the crap out of them.

Gunfire erupted all around us, and we were pinned in our vehicle. A bullet hit my right arm, and it stung like hell. The window was raked with automatic fire from an AK47 just as I ducked below the dash. The bullets pinged against the truck and shattered the windshield.

I felt something warm hit me on the left side of my face and turned to see my dad didn't have a face anymore. A blast of gunfire from inside the truck deafened me. I turned and saw Pat and Darla shooting back at the moonshiners. I was in shock and denial as I grabbed Dad's pistol, opened the door, and shoved it outward. I rolled on the ground, and low crawled a few feet until I had a clear line of fire. I started shooting, and people fell. I was blind with rage and killed everything in sight. Something hit my chest like a sledgehammer and knocked me backward. I ignored the pain and charged forward. Lucky for me, there were no kids at the BBQ. I would have killed them in my blood lust.

The shooting from the truck slacked off, and there was only a shot every now and then. The asshats thought my bullets were coming from the inside of the truck, so they concentrated their fire on the truck. By the time, the fight was over, there were fourteen men and eight women lying dead on the ground. I saw one crawling to get away and placed a well-aimed bullet in his butt. My body armor saved my life twice that day because another round struck me before I could kill the last of them.

I walked through the dead and dying and didn't shoot any of them to put them out of their suffering. I took their weapons and pitched them off into the weeds. The bastards had killed Zack Walker, the best man on the face of the earth and my dad. Several begged for mercy, and I kicked them in the side. I wanted to piss on them, but I heard a feeble cry for help from the ambulance.

"Uncle Jason, help!" cried my nephew, Jerry.

I left the slaughtered men and women and forced the back door open to reveal a grizzly sight. Darla was dead with a bullet hole above her right eye. Pat was slumped over the top of little Sally. She had a huge hole in her back where a large caliber bullet had exited. I rolled her off Sally to see something that chilled me to the bone. My niece had two bloody holes in her chest. She'd died instantly. I can't stand to think about children being hurt in any form or fashion.

I sat there crying with Jerry sitting in my lap. I saw Heather tending to a graze on her left arm and remembered we had to get the heck out of there before someone else came to the sound of the shooting. I gave my nephew to Heather and moved Dad's body to the back.

I held back the tears as my military training kicked in and told me that I had to get the rest of my people away from the carnage. Everyone within a mile had heard the gunfire. The ambulance started, and I drove through the brush back to the highway dodging trees and throwing everyone back and forth in the back.

Heather yelled, "The radiator was shot up! The engine will seize if you keep going!"

"Hang on! We're getting as far from this place as we can before the engine craps out."

We made it several miles before the clunking started. I aimed the truck off the road and into the trees for a second time. I stopped the truck as soon as I couldn't see the road behind us and laid my head on the steering wheel. My eyes watered as I realized that I was responsible for my dad, sister-in-law, and niece's deaths. I was still in a daze but realized that I hadn't seen MMax. I was in a panic. I turned and crawled into the back to find my dog with his head on Jerry's lap. MMax was okay and trying to sooth my nephew.

I patted MMax's head and said, "Good boy."

I tried to sooth Jerry and at the same time, I patted MMax and rubbed his ears. I barely felt Heather tear my sleeve and tend to my wounded arm. I'd lost friends in battle before but had never lost someone close to me. My mind was fuzzy and my thinking cloudy when a flash of sanity happened. I had to suck it up and get my nephew and Heather home to safety. I had failed my dad, Pat, Sally, and Darla, but I would not fail these two.

I opened the back doors to the ambulance and said. "Heather, take several of the extra 9mm pistols and ammo. Reload your magazines and prepare to leave here after I bury the others."

I looked my nephew in the eyes. "Jerry, life just dealt us a crap sandwich. We have to shut the tears off for a while and fight back. Help me bury my dad and your mom and sister. You'll have to grow up much faster than any normal eleven-year-old. I need your help. Come on with me."

The boy wiped his eyes and followed me to the driver's side of the ambulance where a shovel was attached to the side. I removed the shovel and started digging three graves. The boy asked, "Don't we need four graves?"

I choked up but said, "I'm burying your sister with your mom, so she won't be lonely. Is that okay?"

He said, "Yes, and please let me dig for a while."

While he dug, I carried the bodies to the gravesite. An hour later, they were in the ground, and we said prayers over them. Heather had packed three backpacks with food, ammunition, and survival gear. I looked at my nephew and handed him a loaded Sig 9mm saying, "I know you can shoot. I also know that I helped your dad teach you gun safety. This is your gun. Don't draw it or point it at anyone unless you intend to kill them. Kill anyone threatening the people you love."

I took the time to show Jerry more about his new Sig and how to safely load and handle the weapon. Heather's face turned red, and she dragged me off to the side. "Jason, he's just a boy and …"

I placed my hands on her shoulders. "Heather, Darla is dead, his grandfather is dead, his mom is dead, and his sister is dead. I want him to have a fighting chance if we run into trouble. He has to grow up and be ready to defend himself."

Heather avoided me as much as possible on the rest of the trip to my home.

I looked back as MMax, and I led them away from my father's grave. I vowed to visit it once a year and always bring Mom with me. At the time, I thought that day was the worst day of my life, and things would get better. They didn't.

★

Chapter 21

The Walker place, Walter Hill, Tennessee.

The morning started before the sun came up as usual. A few birds were chirping along with the shrieks of the tree frogs. A raccoon was on top of the garbage can by the barn stymied by the tarp strap that held the lid on. A dog barked, and Kat's eyes opened. She sniffed the air as MMax had done so many times when he'd led Jason and her to safety. The fragrance was powerful and beckoned her. Kat stumbled out of bed and walked to the kitchen in her shorts and one of Jason's huge t-shirts that hung loosely from her slender body. "Coffee, I smell coffee. Is it someone's birthday?"

Jan and Michelle raised their cups. "Serve yourself, if you can open your eyes long enough," Michelle said.

Jan chuckled and patted Kat on the back as she passed them. "Our men should be back any day now. I feel it in my bones."

"It was cool last night for the first time since spring. I sure could have snuggled up to Jason to keep me warm. I miss him."

Jan had a thoughtful expression on her face. "My Zack keeps me warm when it's cold outside. My feet are cold, and he lets me put them between his legs to warm them. He'd better get back before it gets cold."

Kat said, "Tina used to snuggle up to me at night, and now she stays in the barn with her pups. By the way, I want the one that has Tina's body and long ears but has MMax's colors. I know he looks a bit weird, but I fell in love with him at first sight."

Jan laughed. "You do know Jason owns both dogs and I guess you have a claim on Jason, so it's us who need to ask you for a pup."

Kat said, "You know Jason wants you two to have any of the pups you want. I suspect that Zack will want one. Back to the cold feet discussion, I want my Jason back because a dog can warm your back, but a man can warm your soul."

No one said anything while Kat poured her coffee. They knew if the men didn't come back in the next few weeks, the chances of them ever returning dropped every day afterward.

Kat sipped her steaming cup of black coffee and sat down at the table. Jan and Michelle joined her. Kat said, "Mom, Michelle, mornings with you two are very special to me. I would probably be dead now, if it weren't for Jason and my two special women. Living alone and having to fight every day for survival is no way of life, and you can't have a long life. Thanks for taking me into your lives."

Later that morning, Jan felt a cold chill run down her spine and attributed it to old age. She'd always heard old people's blood was thin and they hated the cold. She loved snow and had even talked Zack into taking her to a fancy ski resort one winter. She looked across the front yard into the woods and hoped Zack and Jason would come down the driveway with Michael and his family. She'd watched for them every day for the past three weeks. She knew they couldn't rush but also knew if they didn't find their loved ones on the way up along the highway, they would never be found. Searching for them away from the road would be long and arduous. It would also expose them to dangers beyond belief. She almost wished they hadn't left the farm.

By late afternoon, everyone had completed their chores and went to their classes. Maria conducted a course in hand-to-hand fighting, which Jan, Michelle, and Kat attended along with five of the others. Murph led a lesson in how to move and shoot using a couple of pellet rifles. Father James turned out to be proficient with a pellet gun, but Sister Grace wouldn't even touch a pellet rifle.

During their break, Jan addressed the group. "I have to say I'm very impressed with our progress. As soon as Jason and my husband get back, we need to intensify our training."

Several folks groaned. "I know. I know, but remember we have also been very successful with our gardens and small crops. This will be the first winter since the disaster, and people will be starving. We will have to protect our farm and prevent them from taking our food."

Sister Grace said, "Can't we share with them. I'd hate to think little kids would starve because we won't share our bounty."

Kat stood up and spoke. "I don't like to talk in front of a crowd, but anyone out there could have worked as hard as you did since the crap hit the fan. Most didn't. If you start giving food away, others will hear about it and soon this place will be overrun by starving people, drug addicts, and thugs. The farm will be ruined, and we will be dead or driven from this place of refuge. Jan owns this place. She has been very

Christian like in bringing in as many people as she has. Most people wouldn't have done as much."

Kat sat down, and there was silence. Jan walked over to Kat and patted her on the back. "I'm sorry, but Kat is right. We're helping all of the people we can now. Zack and I plan to add Michael and his family plus two more families during the next year. We will expand the farm out to include any abandoned property, but the larger we grow, the larger the target we become. Never, ever, mention our farm to outsiders. We can't help anyone if this is taken from us."

***

Ray saw them having their meeting and put the first step of his plan in motion. He knew that damned dog was in the barn and he wanted the dog to chase him, so he made sure he approached with the wind blowing upwind from him to the barn. He stopped several times along the way to listen for barking. He didn't want the dog to catch him by surprise and have to fight it off. He stopped about a hundred yards away so he could stay ahead of the vicious mutt. He was about to give up when he saw the barn door open slightly and heard the dog barking. He took off, running for his blind.

He arrived at his tree stand a couple of minutes before the dog burst through the tall grass. He was ready and raised his compound bow. He drew the bow back and took aim. The dog was only thirty feet away, and the arrow's flight was accurate. The arrow pierced the dog below the front shoulder and through the lungs. Tina looked up at the man and growled. His was the last face she ever saw.

Ray laughed as the liver and white Springer Spaniel writhed in pain before becoming lifeless. He picked the dog's carcass up in his arms and carried it away from the cabin down below. He saw some thick brush and hid it. He walked away thinking about the next phase of his plan. Now, he could sneak up on the others without that pesky dog biting at him and alerting the others.

***

The morning was colder than expected, and I missed Kat lying next to me. MMax was warm against my side, but it wasn't the same. I rolled over, and MMax laid his muzzle on my chest. I scratched his ears and behind his head. I wrapped my arm around his neck and gave him a gentle hug. He pulled his head out of my grasp as if to say, *"Don't get too emotional with me."* I couldn't help it because I loved my dog as much as most people loved their kids.

The sun was barely showing above the tree line, and I rose from my pile of leaves even though my feet and legs still hurt from two days of walking. I was in great physical shape, though I was an emotional wreck. MMax stood beside me for a second then ran over to a tree to do his part in watering the vegetation. I said, "MMax, watch them," and walked into the brush to perform my morning ritual.

The air was thick with a dense fog, since the ground was much warmer than the air around Percy Priest Lake. Without the fake hazmat truck, we couldn't drive down the road as if we owned it. I decided to head east, which would allow us to walk the back streets through LaVergne and Smyrna to my folk's home.

I stood there looking down at Jerry and Heather as I yawned and stretched. The one thing I liked about the apocalypse was there was silence. Well, I loved the absence of machinery and human noise. It wasn't silent at all, if you listened. A whippoorwill belted out a tune over by the lake accompanied by tree frogs. A couple of crickets chirped down by the creek, and an owl hooted somewhere in the distance. The sounds almost took my mind off the deaths of my family and a new friend. The thoughts pissed me off, and I yelled for the others to get up and prepare to leave.

Later that day, Heather and Jerry were tired. "Jason, Jerry, and I are exhausted. I know we're only four or five miles from your place, but we can't walk any further. We've been walking since five o'clock, and it's now three. We're not soldiers," Heather said, and then she plopped down on the side of the road. Jerry joined her and then both looked up at me with dirty faces.

"Look, the longer it takes to walk home, the more we're exposed to danger. I can't lose any more of my friends and loved ones."

Heather said, "Jason, we get it. We do, but we're exhausted and need to rest. If you go on, we're staying here until the morning. Let's get up early and head to your place."

"Okay, I know when to retreat. Let me go check out that building over there and see if we can stay there for the night. It looks like rain clouds are blowing in on us."

Jerry said, "Thanks, Uncle Jason. I'm worn out."

I told them to hide in the bushes while I checked out the building. I walked around the perimeter of the structure and found it to be an older cinder block building with a huge pole barn added to the back. The front of the building had a brick façade and a fancy sign that said "VFW and Post 1234."

I didn't see anyone around, so I peeked into several of the windows. One in the back was already broken. The front part of the building was a bar and meeting place for veterans and their guests. I tried the door and found it was locked. This surprised me because most buildings had been ransacked by now. I tried the other doors and found the other two locked as well. That left only one thing to do.

I went to the window in the back and caught a whiff of a rotten odor. Then I reached in and raised the window, so I could get in without being cut. The familiar stench of rotting bodies hit me hard. I backed up and tried not to puke my dang guts out. I pulled out a handkerchief, wet it from my water bottle, and tied it over my mouth and nose. The stink was horrible but bearable to me.

I pulled myself through the window and raised the blinds on the other windows to reveal a mass murder. Men, women, and children were strewn around the room. There were no signs of foul play except the dried white froth on their mouths. I was sure the glasses on the table contained cyanide. I guessed they couldn't face the apocalypse and tricked the kids into drinking the poison first, and then committed mass suicide.

I left the large room containing over fifty bodies and now knew why no one had tried to enter the building. They'd all looked through the broken window and gagged. I had the misfortune to have been around death and dying for over four years. I was used to the stench of a bloated, rotten body.

I explored the rest of the building and only found a few pistols, a bottle of whiskey, and some candy bars. I walked out the front door and saw a small pavilion that overlooked Percy Priest Lake. From there, I saw a couple of houseboats floating in a cove. I checked them out and found them deserted. We could spend the night there.

***

The sun had set below the trees, and several of the team sat on the deck with Jan, Michelle, and Kat. The ladies reminisced about the days before the grid went down and what they missed the most. Maria and Pete walked up to them. "Karen, get your partner and take your turn. Hey, has anyone seen Tina? I saw one of the puppies wandering out behind the barn."

Karen responded, "I'll get Murph and be ready in five minutes. We'll keep an eye out for Tina while we make our rounds. She probably went rabbit hunting."

Kat was mad at herself for not noticing Tina was missing. "Jan, please look after the puppies, and Billie and I will go look for Tina. Karen is probably right about Tina going rabbit hunting, but I have a creepy feeling that someone has been watching us for quite a while. Tina looks into the woods and barks but never wants to leave her pups."

Karen fetched her rifle and joined Murph as they took their turn walking the perimeter of the farm while Father James and Sister Grace watched over the house and barn. Karen heard something rustle in the bushes. "Murph, I think a deer just ran into the brush over there. Let's check it out."

Murph's training kicked in, and he said, "Not so fast. I've seen the enemy make a noise just to lure us into an ambush. Let's take our time and keep an eye out for strangers. I'll take the point, and you watch our rear and the left. I'll take the right side. Let's go."

They walked a few yards into the thick brush and heard the sound of twigs breaking. Murph was alarmed. "Ambush. Duck and cover. Be ready to …"

Karen heard Murph crash to the ground ahead of her and stumbled and then fell as she tripped on him in the dark. Murph tried to speak but only made a gurgling sound with the arrow sticking through the front of his neck. Karen leaned over him and felt the arrow. She smelled Ray's tobacco breath coming from behind her.

Before she could react, she felt a blow to the back of her head and darkness washed over her as she felt herself being dragged through the bushes. She blacked out and didn't feel her body being thrown into the back of the truck.

Ray giggled and couldn't contain his glee. He had one woman and now to obtain Billie and perhaps some other women and girls to sell or trade with the Nashville and Lebanon gangs. The first part of his plan had worked to perfection, the woman called Karen was bound and gagged in the back of his truck. Now, he had to get five or six more. He drooled when he thought about Karen's two girls and the small blonde-haired woman. He wanted them the most after Billie, but any of the women would do. The gangs liked the young ones but traded for any good-looking women.

Ray checked his pistol and then hefted his bow and quiver. The bow had three arrows in its rack, and he had a dozen more in the quiver. He walked toward the barn and saw the priest and nun guarding the buildings. He didn't want to alert them, so he drifted behind the barn and walked around it to see the front of the house. He heard their voices first, and laughed to himself as they called out to that damned dead dog.

Ray slipped back into the woods and searched the darkness for the women calling for the dog. He was lucky. He saw the blonde and one of the other women. It was the woman he wanted the most, Billie. The other women were attractive, and Ray could trade them for some valuable supplies. He wanted to keep Billie for himself. He knew he could only handle one at a time, so he had to separate them. He watched as they walked along the woods and noticed they were heading his way. The small blonde was in the lead with Billie several steps behind her.

He lowered his bow and took his billy club from his belt. He waited until the blonde passed him and then stepped out behind Billie. He reached around her and cupped his hand over her mouth as he brought the club down on her head. She went limp in his arms, and he laid her on the ground.

Ray walked quickly up behind the blonde woman and was ready to attack her when she suddenly turned. Ray swung the club and knocked the gun from her hand. She kicked him in the shin and threw herself at him, pummeling him enough that he was scared. He punched her on the side of the head, and she dropped to the ground. His leg and arms ached from the beating, but he grinned when he thought about what he'd do to the girl before he traded her to the gangs.

Ray easily carried Kat to the truck and dumped her in on top of Karen. He went back and picked Billie up. She was much heavier than the tiny Kat, so he struggled to get back to the truck. Ray was now exhausted and decided to cut his losses and leave now. He saw lights all around the house and barn and knew it would be dangerous to try to capture any more women.

He rested for a few minutes and lifted Billie into the bed of the truck. He'd just finished dropping her limp body on top of the others when he heard someone crashing through the brush and tall grass. Ray hid behind a nearby tree until he saw two forms emerge from the brush and run to the back of the truck.

Missy said, "There's someone in the back of the truck. Bring your flashlight."

Chrissy ran up to the truck with her flashlight shining on the bed. "Oh, my God, it's Kat and Billie. They must be dead. Hey, there's another woman below …"

Missy saw her mom's face. "It's mom. Mom, are you okay?"

Ray jumped out from behind a tree and clubbed Missy from behind. He then knocked Chrissy to the ground and tied her hands and feet. "Stay there, or I'll kill you," Ray said as he lifted Missy up and placed her into the back of the truck."

He turned to Chrissy, and something hit him in the back, knocking him down. Kat had untied her feet but couldn't get the knot on her wrists untied. She'd hit him in the back with her shoulder and knocked him down. She began kicking him with all her might. "Untie yourself and go get help!" Kat said as she landed a blow to Ray's head.

Ray was dazed but saw Chrissy get up and run away. He couldn't lose any more of the women, and this one was going to kick him to death. He reached behind him as another vicious kick caught him in the groin. He yanked the gun toward Kat and pulled the trigger three times before she fell to the ground. Ray didn't check to see if she was dead because he heard people yelling behind him. He started the truck and drove as fast as he could away from there. He was in such a hurry that he'd forgotten to put the tailgate up. The truck bounced high when Ray ran over a small downed tree, and Missy and Billie fell to the forest floor. The truck was back at Ray's place before he found he only had Karen.

Ray chained her beside Sister Joan and inspected his wounds. His kneecap was dislocated, and his ribs were broken. He knew he would get even with that blonde wildcat but not today. He was pissed that he'd lost the woman he'd most wanted, but these would do for now.

★

Chapter 22

Percy Priest Lake, Tennessee.

We spent the night on the most luxurious boat I could imagine. Of course, all the food and liquor had been pilfered months ago, but the beds were fantastic. I slept the best I had since leaving Mom and Dad's place. That made me think about my dad, and tears welled up in my eyes. I know it was just dumb luck for us to have crashed that party starting the gunfight, but I still felt responsible for his death.

I searched both boats while the others prepared to leave. I thought the vessels had been picked clean until I tripped and fell against one of the cabin walls below deck. I fell back to the bed and saw the wall open. It was a hidden door to a secret room. There was a steel door behind the wood. It was a safe room. Then I saw the contents, and it wasn't a safe room. It was a drug smuggler's hidden compartment.

There was a stack of brick-like shapes that were all wrapped in duct tape. I cut one open, and white powder fell out. Even a clueless guy like me knew enough about drugs to know this was most likely cocaine. Next to the drugs was a pallet of more brick-like items. I knew exactly what these bricks were. One hundred dollar bills. My mind was blown away by the sheer amount of money. There must have been fifty to one hundred million dollars in this room. The amazement washed away when I saw MMax take a leak on the corner of the pallet of money. Then I realized I couldn't eat it or trade it for anything. Money was worthless these days. I tucked a bundle in my shirt, so the team would believe me. I started to leave when I saw the stack of old ammo boxes.

The first was heavy, so I opened it. It was full of gold coins. Two of the boxes contained gold, and the other three had silver coins. Now I was rich. I took the boxes off the boat and buried them in the woods where I could come back later and get them. I did stick five of each in my pockets.

We were only a few miles from home, so I asked Jerry and Heather to pick up the pace so we could be there before lunch. They were still tired, and Jerry had blisters on his feet. We took many breaks and still made it to the driveway to our home before eleven o'clock. I saw Father James and one of the women we had rescued guarding the front of the house. I waved at him as soon as we started walking down the driveway. He waved back and then dropped to his knees and prayed. That didn't seem off to me, but Tina not running out to meet us was.

Father James jumped up and ran to me. "Jason, where is Zack? Are you okay? Kat's been shot."

"Whoa, back up. Did you say Kat's been shot?"

"Yes, someone abducted several of the women, and Kat was shot trying to save them. Go to your mom."

I dropped my rifle and backpack and ran into the house, nearly knocking my mom to the floor. "Mom, where is Kat?"

"Son, she's in your room. Follow me. We're doing the best we can, and if she doesn't get an infection, we think she'll live."

I walked past Mom and barged into the room. Chrissy and Michelle were tending to Kat. Kat lay on her back with her shoulder bandaged and her leg up on a pillow. It also was wrapped in a bandage. I kneeled down beside her and kissed her on her cheek. Tears flowed freely as I tried to think. "What happened?"

Chrissy said, "We think it was Ray. You know, the man who stalked Billie and Mark right after the world collapsed. Kat helped me escape and kicked the crap out of Ray, so he shot her. He was in such a hurry to escape that he didn't close his tailgate. Billie and Missy fell off the truck."

MMax ran into the room and barked. I ran him out of the room. I didn't have time for a silly dog.

Chrissy broke into tears and couldn't speak. Michelle said, "Ray still has Karen. She didn't get thrown from the truck."

I asked, "When did this happen?"

Michelle said, "Last night. Maria and Pete found Missy and Billie still unconscious and bound about a hundred yards northeast of the house. They saw tire tracks leading away."

Chrissy said, "Jason, please go get my mom. Hey, where are your dad and brother?"

I kissed Kat again and wanted to run to my mom, but she walked into the room with Jerry and Heather. Mom sobbed but tried to console Jerry between bouts of tears.

I wiped tears from my eyes. "Mom, I'm so sorry. It was my fault."

Mom looked up as she sniffled and dried her tears. "Jason, those men who shot at you were at fault along with some bad luck. You killed them all, and that's all you could do. Now, give Kat a kiss and go find that son of a bitch and send him to Hell. Bring Karen back to her family."

I said, "Mom, I can't leave Kat until she recovers. I now know how much she means to me. I can't leave her again."

Then I heard a weak voice. "Do what your mother said. Give me a kiss like you mean it and go kill that bastard who shot me."

"Kat, you're awake," I said as I turned and sat down beside her on the bed.

She said, "Watch bouncing my bed. It hurts me. Now kiss me."

I kissed her and said, "I can't leave you."

"Of course you can. If you don't, that man will come back and finish the job. Can't you see he still wants Billie?"

I kissed her again and said, "Please watch over her until I get back."

I hugged my mom and said, "Michelle, please help Mom and Kat until I get back."

I felt MMax brush against me and then beg me to follow him. He took me to the laundry room and began sniffing Kat's pile of clothes. He sniffed and then barked several times. It suddenly dawned on me that the man had picked Kat up and left his smell on her clothes. MMax was ready to track the man down.

I grabbed my rifle and backpack and yelled to Maria. "Grab your gun and follow MMax!"

MMax ran around the barn to find his mate. An evil smell hit his nose on the backside of the barn. It was the evil one. He had been around the barn. MMax wondered if the evil one was why the humans were so upset. He went in the barn and found Mark and one of the other kids feeding his pups. He sniffed them and then ran to the house to get his human. He knew what direction Tina had gone and wanted his human to help him find Tina.

MMax pawed the screen door open, walked into the house, and again caught a whiff of the evil one's smell. He tested the air until he found the source in the laundry room. The odor was on his human mate's clothes. Now MMax was frantic, so he charged into the bedroom and begged his human to go with him. His human pushed him away. MMax watched the water roll down his human's cheeks and had never seen his human act like this.

***

MMax led us up the hill to the northwest and was more eager than usual. Maria said, "Where's he going? We found Billie and Missy east of here."

"MMax knows what he's doing. Follow him."

MMax howled for the first time ever when tracking an enemy. He broke into some shrubs, and his howl was earsplitting. It unnerved me, and I thought he was crazy until I saw Tina's lifeless body. MMax had his paws on top of her and howled a painful sound. I patted him on the head, and he snapped at me but stopped when he realized it was me. I rubbed his back, and tears came to my eyes as I realized how much Tina had meant to both MMax and me.

Maria stood back and gave us a few minutes, but MMax sniffed Tina's body and then begged me to follow him. We walked north for a while and then turned east. MMax took us to the place where Ray had parked his truck when he'd kidnapped Karen, sniffed around, and then tugged at his leash to head north.

"Maria, we need to be a bit more cautious than usual because MMax is out of his mind with grief and anger."

Maria scowled at me. "Who isn't these days? The SOB killed our friend Murph."

"What?" I came to a stop. In all the turmoil I hadn't noticed that Murph wasn't around. "What happened?"

"Ray shot him with an arrow, so he could disarm Karen and kidnap her. This Ray is either good at killing or lucky."

I said, "Billie told me he was a dumb redneck hillbilly with crap for brains."

Maria said, "I think he's much smarter than that."

"I hope not because if he's that smart, he would have gotten the Hell out of here last night and we'll never find him."

Well, Ray wasn't that smart, or his hormones kept him from leaving. MMax led us to his place, and the truck was parked behind the building. Ray's scent was strong, and it was all I could do to restrain him. I said, "Stay," in my firmest voice before MMax stopped pulling on the leash.

We watched for a minute, and someone opened the door and pitched a couple of backpacks onto the ground. Ray was ready to make his escape. I said, "MMax, heel," and walked to the truck and hid behind it. The door opened again and this time MMax nearly took my arm off when he charged the open door. The leash broke free from my hand, and MMax hit the open door at full speed. We heard screams and then silence, and we ran through the doorway to see MMax had Ray by the neck violently shaking him. Then MMax tumbled away from Ray when a chunk of Ray's throat tore apart. Ray tried to stand with blood running down his chest. MMax jumped on him and knocked him to the floor.

MMax stood on Ray's chest with blood spurting onto him from Ray's throat. Well, what was left of Ray's throat. A large chunk of his throat was still in MMax's mouth. MMax dropped the piece of Ray and kept biting Ray on the face. I said, "Out."

MMax turned to look at me, and it was almost like he had to decide to obey me. MMax wagged his tail and stepped off Ray. Then he did something that made everyone laugh. He hiked his leg and peed on Ray's face.

Maria said, "Good boy."

I said, "MMax, heel."

MMax came over to me, licking the blood from his muzzle. I said, "Good boy."

MMax lay on the ground and watched us cut Karen's bindings. Ray had molested her, and it took years for her and the others that had been assaulted by Ray to recover to a healthier state of mind. I checked the place for anything we could use, but Karen yelled, "Burn it all down around the bastard!"

I found a can of gas and doused Ray's body and the walls before stepping out of the building. I dipped a stick into the gas, lit it, and tossed it into the building. It was fully engaged in a few minutes. Karen had a faint smile. Ray's reign of terror was over.

***

MMax saw the open door, and the smell of the evil one was intense. He took off and felt the leash yank him back for a second, and then he was free. He hit the doorway on the run. An oil lamp allowed him to see Ray as he raised the knife to kill Karen. Karen tried to kick Ray's feet out from under him, but her feet were bound. Karen closed her eyes, so she wouldn't see the knife plunging toward her.

MMax had vengeance on his mind and hate in his heart when he bypassed the man's arm and went for his throat. He shook his head as his teeth sunk into Ray's neck. MMax bit with as much power as he could muster. The evil one would never harm his family or the humans again.

***

We helped Karen into the front seat with Maria while MMax and I rode in the bed. I wiped his muzzle off so he wouldn't scare people back at the farm. He laid beside me with his head on my lap. I wondered if I could ever control MMax again. I trusted him and knew he wouldn't harm my friends or me, but he was loose cannon.

We never discovered what had happened to Sister Joan. Her body was never found.

MMax jumped out of the truck before it stopped and turned to me for approval. He then ran in the barn when I said, "Go."

I looked in the barn, and he lay beside his pups, licking them. I knew he would be a good father, even though he had become so vicious with evil people. I saw a lot of me in him. Just because a man has to kill bad people doesn't make him a bad dog or person.

I helped Karen into the house and then saw Mom watching us. "Son, is it over? I can't stand much more."

I cringed and didn't want to say anything. "Mom, this chapter is over, but there will be many more challenges. That guy they call the General will have to be dealt with before he overruns our farm."

"Can't we flee to a safer place?"

"No, we can't. There are generals in every area. You have to squash them like bugs every time you find one."

I gave Mom a kiss on top of her head and then went to our room. Michelle left as I laid down beside Kat. I tried not to wake her up, but her eyes popped open. "Is he dead?"

"Yes, and it was a gruesome death."

"Did you slit his throat?"

"No, I didn't kill him."

"Maria?"

"No, babe, MMax killed him. The bastard killed Tina before he started the attack. MMax ripped his throat out and pissed on his head."

Kat turned her head, and we kissed, and she asked, "Does this mean …?

"Yes," I said as I kissed her.

Then she said, "Remember that puppy with Tina's body and MMax's color?"

I replied, "Yes, I do. The one you wanted?"

"Yes, I want you to start training him to be MMax junior. I know he's not a Belgium Malinois, but he'll be mine and can protect me when you're gone."

I said, "MMax takes a firm hand. Will you be up to it?

"I caught and tamed you."

"Yes, dear."

Kat kissed me. "See? You can be trained. Jason, the crap is still hitting the fan and won't stop anytime soon. I never want to have a man overpower me again. I want you to take up where Zack left off and train us ladies to be **Amazon Warriors**."

The End

of

War Dogs

No One Left Behind

*

Thanks for reading War Dogs: No One Left Behind, and please don't forget to give it a great review on Amazon. Book 3 should be published by the end of fall 2019.

*I kinda like the title "War Dogs **Amazon Warriors**" for the title of Book 3. We'll see.*

Remember to read my other books on Amazon.

AJ Newman

If you like my novel, please post a review on Amazon.

To contact or follow the Author, please leave comments at:
https://www.facebook.com/newmananthonyj/

To view other books by AJ Newman, go to Amazon to my Author's page:
http://www.amazon.com/-/e/B00HT84V6U

A list of my other books follows at the end.

Thanks, AJ Newman

Books by AJ Newman

War Dogs
Heading Home
No One Left Behind
Amazon Warriors (late fall 2019)

EMP:
Perfect Storm
Chaos in the Storm

Cole's Saga series:
Cole's Saga
FEMA WARS

American Apocalypse:
American Survivor
Descent Into Darkness
Reign of Darkness
Rising from the Apocalypse

After the Solar Flare:
Alone in the Apocalypse
Adventures in the Apocalypse

Alien Apocalypse:
The Virus
Surviving

A Family's Apocalypse Series:
Cities on Fire
Family Survival

The Day America Died:
New Beginnings

Old Enemies
Frozen Apocalypse

The Adventures of John Harris:
Surviving
Hell in the Homeland
Tyranny in the Homeland
Revenge in the Homeland
Apocalypse in the Homeland
John Returns

AJ Newman and Mack Norman
Rogue's Apocalypse:
Rogues Origin
Rogues Rising
Rogues Journey

A Samantha Jones Murder Mystery:
Where the Girls Are Buried
Who Killed the Girls?

AJ Newman and Cliff Deane:
Terror in the USA: Virus: Strain of Islam

These books are available on Amazon:
https://www.amazon.com/AJ-Newman/e/B00HT84V6U/ref=dp_byline_cont_ebooks_1

To contact the Author, please leave comments at:
www.facebook.com/newmananthonyj

*

About the Author

AJ Newman is the author of 29 science fiction and mystery novels and 7 audiobooks that have been published on Amazon and Audible. He was born and raised in a small town in the western part of Kentucky. His Dad taught him how to handle guns very early in life, and he and his best friend Mike spent summers shooting .22 rifles and fishing.

Reading is his passion, and he read every book he could get his hands on. He fell in love with science fiction. He graduated from USI with a degree in Chemistry and made a career working in manufacturing and logistics, but always fancied himself as an author.

He served six years in the Army National Guard in an armored unit and spent six years performing every function on M48 and M60 army tanks. This gave him great respect for our veterans who lay their lives on the line to protect our country and freedoms.

He currently resides in a small town just outside of Owensboro, Kentucky with his wife Patsy and their four tiny Shih Tzu's, Sammy, Cotton, Callie, and Benny. All except Benny are rescue dogs.

Made in the USA
Las Vegas, NV
29 March 2022

46538053R00173